IS TASHA GOOD ENOUGH?

Fighting back tears of rage and frustration, Tasha marched over to Orchid. She turned away as the thin girl, still dressed in a gold two-piece outfit with a bare midriff, flipped through the sketches.

"Mmmm . . . nice . . . oh . . . oh, dear—"

Tasha had had enough. "Give me that!" she demanded, grabbing her portfolio.

"You have one or two good pieces," Orchid said. "I liked the shoulder lines in particular, but the rest of it is a little . . . ordinary. Don't you think so?"

Tasha gave her an icy stare.

18 Pine St.

Fashion by Tasha

Written by
Stacie Johnson

Created by
WALTER DEAN MYERS

A Seth Godin Production

BANTAM BOOKS

NEW YORK · TORONTO · LONDON · SYDNEY · AUCKLAND

RL 5, age 10 and up

FASHION BY TASHA
A Bantam Book / May 1993

*Thanks to Susan Korman, Betsy Gould, Amy Berkower, Fran Lebowitz, Marva Martin,
Michael Cader, Margery Mandell, José Arroyo, Julie Maner, Kate Grossman,
Ellen Kenny, and Lucy Wood.*

18 Pine St. is a trademark of Seth Godin Productions, Inc.

ISBN 0-553-29724-4

Published simultaneously in the United States and Canada

Bantam Books are published by Bantam Books, a division of Bantam Doubleday
Dell Publishing Group, Inc. Its trademark, consisting of the words "Bantam
Books" and the portrayal of a rooster, is Registered in U.S. Patent and
Trademark Office and in other countries. Marca Registrada. Bantam Books, 1540
Broadway, New York, New York 10036.

PRINTED IN THE UNITED STATES OF AMERICA

0 9 8 7 6 5 4 3 2 1

For Kate

18 Pine St.

There is a card shop at 8 Pine Street, and a shop that sells sewing supplies at 10 Pine that's only open in the afternoons and on Saturdays if it doesn't rain. For some reason that no one seems to know or care about, there is no 12, 14, or 16 Pine. The name of the pizzeria at 18 Pine Street was Antonio's before Mr. and Mrs. Harris took it over. Mr. Harris removed Antonio's sign and just put up a sign announcing the address. By the time he got around to thinking of a name for the place, everybody was calling it 18 Pine.

The Crew at 18 Pine St.

Sarah Gordon is the heart and soul of the group. Sarah's pretty, with a great smile and a warm, caring attitude that makes her a terrific friend. Sarah's the reason that everyone shows up at 18 Pine St.

Tasha Gordon, tall, sexy, and smart, is Sarah's cousin. Since her parents died four years ago, Tasha has moved from relative to relative. Now she's living with Sarah and her family—maybe for good.

Cindy Phillips is Sarah's best friend. Cindy is petite, with dark, radiant skin and a cute nose. She wears her black hair in braids. Cindy's been Sarah's neighbor and friend since she moved from Jamaica when she was three.

Kwame Brown's only a sophomore, but that doesn't stop him from being part of the crew. Kwame's got a flattop haircut and mischievous smile. As the smartest kid in the group, he's the one Jennifer turns to for help with her homework.

Jennifer Wilson is the poor little rich girl. Her parents are divorced, and all the charge cards and clothes in the world can't make up for it. Jennifer's tall and thin, with cocoa-colored skin and a body that's made for all those designer clothes she wears.

Billy Turner is a basketball star. His good looks, sharp clothes, and thin mustache make him a star with the women as well. He's already broken Sarah's heart—and now Tasha's got her eye on him as well.

April Winter has been to ten schools in the last ten years—and she hopes she's at Murphy to stay. Her energy, blond hair, and offbeat personality make her a standout at school.

José Melendez seems to be everyone's friend. Quiet and unassuming, José is always happy to help out with a homework assignment or project.

And there's Dave Hunter, Brian Wu, and the rest of the gang. You'll meet them all in the halls of Murphy High and after school for a pizza at 18 Pine St.

18
PINE

One

"Careful!" Jennifer Wilson cried. She quickly slid to the end of the booth as Sarah Gordon skidded toward their table, barely managing to set down a tray of drinks without spilling them.

"What did I slip on?" asked Sarah. She turned around and saw the french fry smeared on the floor. Kwame Brown and José Melendez, who had a basket of fries between them, were watching her sheepishly.

Sarah's friends from Murphy High had gotten together at 18 Pine St. "just for sodas," but the wonderful smells inside the pizzeria were too hard to resist. They'd ended up ordering an extra-large deep-dish pie. Nobody minded staying inside a little longer. Outside the rain was coming down hard, and if it got any colder, the precipitation would turn to sleet.

As Jennifer smoothed her beige silk blouse, Tasha Gordon pointed her straw at her. "You didn't really think a french fry could interfere with the Gordon coordination, did you?"

"At least you had faith in me, cousin." Sarah laughed as she sat down next to Tasha. "Jennifer thought it was all over for her new blouse."

Although Sarah and Tasha were practically the same age, the cousins couldn't be more different. Tasha's mother and father had been killed in a car accident several years ago and since then, Tasha had lived with one relative after another. Recently Sarah's father had brought Tasha to live with them.

Madison was small compared to Tasha's hometown of Oakland, California, and her big-city background had given Tasha the confidence to take the new place by storm. She had quickly become one of the most outspoken and popular girls in school. Her talent on the basketball court helped make the Murphy High girls' squad a powerhouse in its division. But even when Tasha wasn't doing anything, her smooth light brown complexion and her curly hair, which fell halfway down her back, were guaranteed to make a lot of heads turn. And that was just fine with her.

Everyone who knew Sarah Gordon considered her just as beautiful as her more outgoing cousin.

Her skin was a few shades darker, a rich mahogany, and her eyes were calm and friendly. Sarah was also much more patient and levelheaded than Tasha, which sometimes made the cousins clash. Usually though, they got along just fine.

Cindy Phillips was nodding at Tasha's remark. "The Gordons *are* incredibly coordinated. Sarah probably hasn't dropped anything since she was five years old," she joked.

"What about Kyle Powers two summers ago?" Jennifer teased. "She dropped him pretty fast."

Sarah faked a glare at Jennifer as everybody laughed, but she didn't really mind. Kyle Powers had been centuries ago.

"Am I glad school's out for the day," Tasha said. "When Mrs. Parisi pulled out those quiz papers in history class, I almost had a heart attack!"

"What happened, Tasha?" Jennifer said with a touch of envy. "Did you get an A instead of an A-plus?"

"In case you've been in orbit for the last two weeks, I've got that charity fashion show tonight," Tasha said. "I haven't been able to think about schoolwork or anything else in weeks."

Tasha had learned how to sew from her mother, and her aunt, Sarah's mother, had asked her to design some clothes for a fashion show to benefit Mother Belva's Home for Young Women. Every year the local charity for homeless young women put the show on to raise money. "Since you're

3

always sketching anyway, you might as well make something," Elizabeth Gordon had said. Tasha had pressed Sarah into service as a model for her "collection," which she called KickBacks. She couldn't wait till tonight, to actually hear someone say: "Another bold look from the KickBack Collection by Tasha Gordon." It would be thrilling to see her creations come to life.

"You're all coming tonight, aren't you?" Tasha said, flashing her dazzling smile at each of them. "My aunt is helping to run the thing, so the more people we get, the better."

"Wouldn't miss it for anything!" Kwame gave Tasha a smile. Since she'd arrived in Madison, he'd been one of her biggest fans.

"Except maybe a pizza," said Cindy. Kwame's appetite for pizza was legendary. "And speaking of pizza, what's taking ours so long?"

"Yeah, Kwame's notebook is starting to look good to me," Tasha said.

"José," Jennifer chimed in, "this special order was your idea. What's taking so long?"

José flipped his hair away from his eyes with a shake of his head. Then he held his hand up and frowned in a dead-on imitation of the assistant principal, Mr. Schlesinger. "'You kids can settle down here, or in my office, it's up to you.' Seriously, folks," he went on in his normal voice, "it's worth the wait. You can't rush a work of art, you know."

"I don't want a work of art. I want pizza," said Kwame.

"Here, eat these." José pushed the plate of french fries directly in front of Kwame. He drummed his fingers on the table and flipped his hair out of his eyes again. "If you never had a pizza with jalapeños on it, you'll think you died and went to heaven."

April Winter returned from the rest room, and dropped down next to Kwame. "Are you sure they're not going to be too hot? I had some chili peppers once and they were murder." She shuddered at the memory.

"Jalapeños aren't nearly as bad as chili peppers," José reassured her. "My mother puts jalapeños in everything."

"Everything? Even Jell-O?" April challenged.

"Eew, I don't even want to think about that," Sarah said. She noticed that Kwame was busy writing in his notebook. He had an amazing ability to concentrate no matter where he was.

"Hey, Kwame," said Jennifer, covering up the page of his notebook with her hands, "didn't you hear the bell? School is out." Although Jennifer took school seriously, she couldn't understand why anybody would spend his time writing when he could be hanging out or, better yet, shopping.

Kwame looked up. Cindy, Jennifer, Sarah, and Tasha were looking at him. He adjusted his black-framed glasses and set the notebook in his lap.

"Sorry. I got carried away with this history report," he said with a grin. "It's about blacks who fought in the Revolutionary War."

Jennifer shook her head. "I can't believe that many blacks actually served in that war. They weren't free themselves at the time—why would they fight for America's freedom?"

"Some were forced to. Others earned their freedom by fighting in the war," Kwame replied. "And there were a lot of free blacks, even before the Civil War. Many of them lived in Boston and New York."

"I've never heard of them," Jennifer said, inspecting her nails.

"How about Crispus Attucks?" Kwame asked. "He was the first man to die in the Revolution."

"He's got you there," April said.

"Who asked you?" Jennifer retorted.

April shrugged. She self-consciously played with her hair and looked a little embarrassed.

"Okay, okay," Jennifer said. "So maybe there were some free blacks and one or two of them fought for independence. Why write about them? They're not in any of the books we have at Murphy. Besides, nobody's ever heard of them."

"That's a good reason right there," Kwame said quietly. "Because nobody's ever heard of them."

The group at the table was silent for a second, then everyone said, "Ooooooooh!" and started laughing.

"Well, go ahead, Kwame!" Tasha said, giving him a high-five.

Kwame went on about the different roles played by black people in the Revolution. Some were Minutemen, while others were messengers or servants. "There were even black spies on both sides!" he said.

Mr. Harris, who ran 18 Pine St., placed a stack of plates and napkins on the table, then carefully lowered an enormous aluminum tray. The cheese on the pizza was still sizzling and bubbling. It was dotted with dozens of light green pepper rings. The smell was simply wonderful.

Kwame picked up a slice and tore into it with gusto.

"Hey, José, this stuff isn't half . . ." It was as far as Kwame got. The jalapeño peppers had found their way onto his tongue and he gulped down the bite and grabbed his orange soda with both hands.

Jennifer, who had nibbled carefully at a tiny bit of jalapeño, suddenly gave a little yelp and reached for her cup. Tasha was next, staring at the two of them in amusement until the peppers got to her. She fought to keep her composure, but a light sheen of sweat broke out on her forehead.

"Are you trying to kill us, José?" April gasped. Her blue eyes were teary.

José looked at them, bewildered. "What's wrong?" he said through his pizza.

7

"There's a hole in my mouth, that's what's wrong," Jennifer snapped. She picked up a plastic fork and pushed the jalapeños off her slice and onto José's plate. Everybody else followed suit until the peppers were piled high on his plate. Only Cindy kept hers.

"Pay no attention to them, José," she said. "I think it's delicious." With that, she picked up a jalapeño and put it on her tongue. She chewed slowly. "Mmmmmm."

"No fair, Cindy," said Sarah. "You're from Jamaica. You're used to that jerk sauce and those little yellow peppers I saw at your house."

"Yeah, they're good too," said Cindy. "Next time, we'll try a pizza with those on it."

"Why stop there?" Tasha grumbled. "Let's get a large deep-dish with red ants!"

Sarah laughed and picked up everyone's empty cup. She started for the soda counter, then turned around and sat down again. "Don't look over right away," she said to Cindy, "but who's that with Dave?"

Cindy pretended to stretch, casually turning her head to look. Dave Hunter's attractive profile was visible in the front of the pizzeria. The table he was leaning his elbows on had not been designed with a basketball player in mind; it made him look even taller than his six feet two inches. A tall, extremely thin girl was opposite him, giving him her fullest attention. By now everybody at Sarah's table was looking in that direction. They watched as the girl stirred the straw slowly in her glass and talked to Dave. Sarah and Tasha glanced at each other. *Flirt.*

"Does she go to Murphy?" Sarah whispered.

"No way, she's too old-looking," Cindy replied. Cindy hoped she sounded convincing. Sarah had kept her up late into the night recently, telling her all the fabulous details about a date with Dave. The way this stranger was sending out signals, it looked like trouble.

The girl's hair was cut extremely short, in an almost punk style. She wore enormous hoop earrings that almost touched her shoulders, and a row of glittering diamond studs ran up one earlobe. Tight purple leggings accented the incredible length of her legs. The girls immediately recognized her purple and white warm-up jacket as one from an expensive designer. Whoever this girl was, she had very good taste.

"That's Orchid," April whispered, staring at the strange girl.

Everyone looked at her.

Two

"That girl. The one with Dave Hunter. Her name is Orchid," April repeated.

"Orchid what?" said Tasha.

"Nothing, just Orchid," April said.

"How do you know her?" demanded Sarah. She immediately felt embarrassed at the way the question had come out, but she couldn't help herself. She and Dave lived only a few houses apart, and they had known each other since they were three. Sarah often thought that if she were older she'd probably think of marrying Dave Hunter. But right now she was more than content just dating him—especially since they'd had some hot dates recently.

She looked at the thin girl who was sitting with Dave now. It was obvious that Orchid was attracted to him, but it was hard to tell what Dave was feeling.

"I saw both of them at the Westcove Mall," explained April. She leaned into the table and lowered her voice. Everyone else leaned in too. "I was walking out of Ms. Tique, and I . . ."

"Ms. Tique?" blurted Jennifer. "Did you see that red miniskirt in the window? I'm thinking of getting it for . . ." She stopped when Tasha nudged her.

"Anyway," April continued, "I saw Dave and her walking together and they ran into Billy Turner."

For a second Tasha looked uncomfortable. She had a not-so-secret crush on the captain of the football team. Billy had a not-so-secret crush on almost everybody. He and Tasha had gone out a few times, but he wasn't completely under her spell. Lately they had been spending some time together. The last thing Billy needed now, decided Sarah, was a distraction.

"When Dave introduced the girl to Billy," April went on, "Dave said, 'This is Teri Smith,' and she said, 'Actually, I prefer the name Orchid.' " April giggled. She stole a glance at the girl and then nodded. "That's her, all right. You can't see her very well from here, but she's really good-looking."

At that moment Orchid turned around. Sarah's body tensed. The girl was gorgeous. Her eyes were green and almond-shaped and her skin was the color of light toast. Her lips were full, almost pouting, and painted in a glossy violet hue.

11

José let out a soft whistle between his teeth. "That Orchid sure is in bloom!" he said.

"Oh, eat your jalapeños!" Cindy snapped. Everyone at the table laughed.

"I know she doesn't go to Murphy," said Jennifer. "Do you think she goes to Hamilton?"

Hamilton High School was for students who needed special attention. Some of them had learning troubles, and others had discipline problems. Sarah's father, Donald Gordon, was principal there.

"She's not in school, she's a musician," April said.

"How did you overhear all this?" said Kwame. "Did you plant a bug in her purse?"

"No, I stopped to say hello," April said. "And Billy was just bubbling over, he was so anxious to talk about her."

"So she's a musician?" Sarah prompted her.

"Well, not really," April replied. "She just plays the tambourine, but she does belong to a band, and you've all heard of it."

She pointed at José's chest.

José was wearing a black sweatshirt with a colorful picture of a huge snake wearing a straw hat and chewing a blade of grass. The snake's fat coils were crushing a tractor. Above the picture, in Gothic letters, were the words Snake Farm.

"She plays for Snake Farm?" Kwame said. "She doesn't look like a heavy-metal type."

"Ugh! I don't like her already," Jennifer said.

12

"It's my brother's sweatshirt," José mumbled. "Besides, if she's with Snake Farm, what's she doing in Madison? They don't come to the Armory for another two weeks."

"Don't look at me," said April. "I'm only telling you what I heard."

Cindy wrinkled up her nose. "It sounds like she's just a groupie."

"Yeah, but what a great-looking groupie," José added. "I wouldn't mind . . ." He stopped when he saw Jennifer, April, Sarah, Tasha, and Cindy glaring at him, daring him to finish the sentence. "I know, I know," he said, " 'Eat your jalapeños!' "

Sarah stood and picked up the tray of cups again. She reached Dave's table just as Billy Turner did. "Hi, Dave."

"Oh, Sarah, what's happening?" Dave stood, looking surprised to see her. "I was just about to come over," he said with a smile. "Teri, this is my friend Sarah. Sarah, this is Teri Smith."

"I told you, it's Orchid," the girl said to Dave with mock annoyance. Her voice was low, with a British accent that didn't sound real.

Sarah smiled and offered her hand. Orchid didn't take it. Instead she looked at Sarah with a slight smirk, then flashed her teeth and tried to pass it off as a smile.

An awkward silence followed.

Billy moved his chair closer to Orchid, scraping it

13

across the floor. "Orchid is going to play with Snake Farm," he told Sarah. "Pretty cool, huh?"

"They're picking me up when they play the Armory," Orchid explained sweetly.

Oh yeah? Sarah thought. She was about to say something nasty when Tasha stepped up.

"Sarah, what's keeping you with those sodas?" Sarah was glad to have the interruption. Tasha won't let this girl get to her, she thought.

Tasha looked at Orchid as if noticing her for the first time. She smiled and held out her hand. "I'm Sarah's cousin, Tasha Gordon," she said. Orchid smiled but didn't extend her hand. Tasha stubbornly kept hers out until finally Orchid shook it.

"Billy!" Tasha said, pretending to scold him, "why aren't you at football practice?"

"Coach cut it short on account of the rain," Billy replied. He looked uncomfortable.

But Tasha didn't wait to hear Billy's answer. She turned to Orchid again. "Did I hear Dave say your name was Teri?"

Orchid's eyes flashed, and they seemed to turn a darker shade of green. "I don't go by that name anymore," she said in her British accent. "I've chosen my own. It's Orchid."

But Tasha had turned her attention back to Billy. Sarah realized that Tasha was trying to throw the new girl off balance. It was working.

"Billy," said Tasha, "you *are* going to be at the

fashion show tonight, aren't you?"

Orchid spoke up before Billy had time to open his mouth. "Oh, you're going to be modeling too?" she said.

Tasha feigned boredom. "Yes. I also designed a few pieces for it."

"Maybe I'll be wearing one of them," Orchid said. "Dave and I saw your high school secretary at the mall. She told me I was just the type to replace one of the models who dropped out."

"I don't think you'll be modeling my work," Tasha replied in a kind tone. "My clothes are more for people our age."

Orchid was unfazed. "You're probably right," she said. She leaned back in her chair and played with one earring as she looked at Billy and Dave. "I'll be wearing something for more mature eyes."

She stood up just then, towering above Tasha and Sarah by a good five inches. "Can you take me home, Dave?" she said. She turned to Sarah and Tasha. "I'll see you at the show."

Billy stood as well. "Can you drop me off too?" he asked Dave. "My car is in the shop," he mumbled to Tasha.

Orchid picked up Dave's book bag and headed toward the door. Dave flashed Sarah a quick smile, then went after her. Billy followed.

Sarah and Tasha walked back to their table with the tray of drinks.

"Charming, isn't she?" Tasha said in a British accent.

"Rather," said Sarah, giggling.

The driving rain forced Sarah and Tasha to rush into their house an hour later. Their grandmother, Miss Essie, came downstairs from her room where Sarah guessed she'd been reading a play script.

"Take your shoes off on the mat," she reminded them.

"We would not want to track mud in the house," Tasha said in a British accent. "That would be unseemly."

Miss Essie, who was a professional actress, held her hands to her ears. "You think that's an English accent?" she said. In a perfect Cockney voice she added, "Ye ain't even close, lay-dees!"

Sarah and Tasha's laughter brought Mr. Gordon out of the den. "You girls better get moving," he warned. "Liz is working late on a case that's going to trial tomorrow. She wants you to go to the community center without her. She'll meet you when the show starts."

Tasha ran to her room and removed five outfits from her closet. She had designed, hemmed, and stitched every inch of them herself, and they hadn't turned out half bad. She had created the colorful sundress after seeing some designs at Cindy's and copied the black catsuit and oversized jacket from

16

the hip-hop clothing that was hot on MTV. The sexy safari outfit was inspired by the photographs of supermodel Iman's trip to Ethiopia. The last creation was one that Sarah would be wearing—a red sequined flapper dress. Tasha was proud of each of them, but worried, too. Would the audience like them?

Sarah took a quick shower and waited for Tasha to come down. She went into the kitchen for a glass of water. Her tongue still felt slightly raw from the jalapeños that José had inflicted on them.

As she put the glass in the sink, Sarah thought about Orchid and Dave. They looked good together. They were both tall and lean. She looked down at her own legs. I'm definitely not as leggy, she thought. And not nearly as exotic or tall, either, added a jealous voice inside her.

Sarah went to the phone and picked up the receiver. She pulled aside the curtain that covered the window over the sink. Part of Dave's lawn was visible from that angle. She knew she had acted a little strange at 18 Pine St. Orchid's coolness had totally flustered her. She remembered how casual and indifferent Tasha had acted. She was . . .What was the word? Unflappable. "I'm too *flappable*," Sarah said to herself.

As she listened to the phone ring at the other end of the receiver, Sarah suddenly felt silly. What am I going to tell him, she thought impatiently, that I'm jealous of some girl I don't even know? Who cares about a tambourine player for Snake Farm? Still she let the phone ring. She would ask him about homework, or something. Just hearing his voice would make her feel better.

The phone at the Hunters' house rang four times before a female voice answered. "Hello," the voice said brightly.

Orchid had picked up Dave's phone!

18

Three

The music pulsed and the applause crackled in the large main room of the Madison Community Center. The annual charity fashion show was underway.

Tasha could hear the announcer opening the show. "Mother Belva's Home, a center for homeless young women, is delighted that you could join us here today. All proceeds from the fashion show go to support the good work of the home. So let's get on with it."

Tasha and Sarah were in the community center's kitchen, a room just off the main performance area which was serving as a dressing room for the event. A plump white woman named Holly was in charge of getting the models ready. She insisted that the kitchen door stay closed so that the audience wouldn't be distracted by the noise, but it made the kitchen stuffy and loud. The smell of hair spray nearly killed them all until Holly found the switch for the kitchen's exhaust fans. The air cleared slightly, but the fans added to the din.

Orchid was there, sitting at a table wearing a pink bathrobe and waiting for her turn to go onstage. "She's not even sweating," Sarah murmured to Tasha.

"Ignore her," said Tasha. "And stop squirming." Tasha adjusted the hem of the red flapper dress she had made, while trying to double-check the black catsuit she had on. "When you're out there, throw your shoulders back and shake your hips. I want this dress to dance!"

The girl who had just been on the runway came into the room. A gust of fresh air blew in with her. "It's a madhouse out there," she declared. "They're eating it up."

"Perfect," Holly said. "Let's keep it up. Where's Sarah Gordon?" she said, looking at her list. "She's on next."

Sarah's heart started pounding. Tasha squeezed her hand and whispered, "You'll do fine."

Tasha held open the kitchen door as Sarah stepped out toward the runway. The music was playing so loudly, she had trouble remembering what Tasha had told her to do. "How did I get into this?" she asked herself as she climbed the stairs to stand behind the curtain. She took several deep breaths while she waited for her music cue. When it came, Sarah took a final sharp breath, pulled the curtains apart, and stepped through.

The crowd applauded enthusiastically as she strolled down the runway. She tried to keep her shoulders straight and her attitude cool. The dress seemed to bounce and shimmer without her help, but she threw her hips slightly to make the beads and sequins glitter even more.

". . . Sarah Gordon's stunning dress will turn heads at any gathering," the announcer said. "The silk and rayon blend is light and comfortable all evening long. The hat and the handbag complement the look. From the KickBack Collection by Tasha Gordon . . ."

Sarah reached the end of the runway and walked to the left. She held the pose for two seconds, then walked to the right. The crowd applauded again.

It was over before Sarah knew it. The music was winding down as she sauntered toward the curtains, her dress rippling with every step. Off to one side she caught a glimpse of Dave. He was applauding wildly and mouthing the word "beautiful."

It's over, Sarah thought. No more nightmares about tripping, or walking down the runway with nothing on. She relaxed her shoulders and let the relief wash over her. She had worried about this night ever since she'd given in to Tasha's pleas and agreed to model.

Tasha ran to her. She gave Sarah a warm hug, then pulled back quickly to smooth her catsuit.

"What did you do out there," Tasha whispered excitedly, "hand out hundred-dollar bills? They were going crazy!"

"What can I say? They loved the dress!" said Sarah. "Now it's your turn to knock them dead."

"Well, here I go," said Tasha determinedly.

A new song came over the loudspeakers and Tasha ran up the stairs to wait for her cue behind the curtain. The cue came and Sarah watched her cousin step out to a blast of hollers and cheers.

Holly had asked the models to go back into the kitchen once their part in the show was over, but when Sarah opened the kitchen door, she noticed that Holly wasn't there. She shut the door again and crept to a spot where she could watch her cousin without being noticed.

". . . Tasha Gordon is ready for summer in the city in this bold catsuit. The cotton fabric is just the thing for those long hot days, and the matching jacket makes it perfect for those even hotter nights. From the Kick-Back Collection by Tasha Gordon . . ."

Moments later Tasha reappeared on Sarah's side of the curtain. Her smile was radiant.

"You really took it to them," Sarah said, giving her cousin a hug.

"Yes, they loved it. I'm very impressed," said a British–accented voice.

Sarah and Tasha were startled at the sound of Orchid's voice. They were even more surprised when they saw what she was wearing.

Orchid had come out of the dressing room in a tiny gold lamé bikini and matching gold beach sandals. She held a light blue beach towel in her hand, which she proceeded to wrap around her shoulders as she climbed the stairs. Tasha and Sarah couldn't help staring. Orchid's build was thin, but not bony. Her chest was bigger than it had appeared in the loose warm-up jacket earlier that day. And her legs seemed to go on forever.

Sarah and Tasha had almost reached the dressing room when Orchid walked through the curtain. She hadn't waited for her musical cue—she'd simply stepped out. The cousins heard the crowd go silent. It was as if the whole audience had inhaled at once. They erupted just as suddenly with an explosion of cheers and clapping. Several men howled and whistled. The announcer's voice was completely lost.

Tasha and Sarah sneaked around the curtain and looked out. If Teri Smith, alias Orchid, had looked gorgeous in the pizzeria, she was dazzling on the runway.

She walked down the runway with the towel wrapped around her. When she reached the end, she pulled off the towel and struck a pose. The yelling and the hooting immediately began again.

Billy Turner, Sarah noticed, was acting like the biggest fool of them all. When Orchid pulled one strap of the bikini top off her shoulder, he stood up and yelled his approval. Orchid smiled at him as she made her final return walk down the runway. Billy stood up and applauded her. Then he got two of his football buddies up out of their seats, but at least it didn't turn into a full standing ovation. Sarah was especially glad that Dave stayed in his seat—until she saw Billy say something that made Dave laugh. Then the two of them exchanged high-fives.

Orchid's bathing suit was not the last piece in the show, but it might as well have been. The crowd clapped politely for the next model, but no one could match Orchid's display. In fact it was almost quiet in the room until she appeared again to close the show. This time Orchid came out in a wedding dress, followed by six bridesmaids. Clear sequins were laced throughout the veil, which she lifted from her face slowly and dramatically in the finale.

After the show, Sarah and Tasha came out of the dressing room and found Kwame, Jennifer, and April waiting for them along with Mrs. Gordon and Allison, Sarah's younger sister. Sarah was glad to see her mother had made it, after all the work she'd done to get ready for the show. Sometimes it felt like Mrs. Gordon was always doing something: arguing a case in court or doing community work. No one was prouder of her mother's career than Sarah, but sometimes she wondered what it would be like to have a mother at home all the time, like Dave Hunter's.

"You guys were great!" Allison said.

"I couldn't have done it without my lovely assistant," Tasha said, bowing.

"I thought the KickBack Collection was the highlight of the evening," Mrs. Gordon said.

"You just *have* to help me make that catsuit," April said.

"It would look great on you, girl," Tasha agreed.

"I'll bet Mother Belva's Home cleaned up tonight," Kwame added. "This place was packed."

"Every bit helps," Mrs. Gordon said. "The women who stay at the home are getting another chance at a good life because of the money we raise. This charity show has become quite a hit. I saw a lot of faces I didn't recognize. And who was that skinny model in the bikini? I thought that was in poor taste."

Allison nudged her mother. "Here she comes."

They all turned to see Dave, Billy, and Orchid making their way through the mob of men and boys who wanted to congratulate her and get her phone number. Now she was wearing a pair of pink denim pants and a pale pink top. Even the diamond studs in her ears reflected pink. All that's missing is a big pink wig, Sarah thought.

"That was quite a bikini you were wearing," Mrs. Gordon commented to Orchid after they had been introduced.

"Wasn't it?" said Orchid. "Back in California I used to wear one just like it." She glanced at Billy for a second. "Of course," she added with a giggle, "in California, I don't usually wear the top part."

Dave pulled Sarah aside. "Congratulations on tonight," he said.

"Thanks," Sarah replied. "It was fun to do—once. I . . . I tried to call you tonight but you must have been busy."

"I was home," Dave said. "Nobody told me you called."

"It was nothing important," said Sarah. She hesitated. "Actually, I was surprised to hear Orchid answer the phone."

"Yeah, I'll bet you were," Dave said with a grin. "She's taken over the house. But don't worry, she's only staying with us while she's in town."

"She's staying at your place?" Sarah couldn't believe it. "How come?"

"Remember my father's friend—the one I stayed with in California?" Dave asked.

Sarah nodded.

"Teri is his daughter. I hung out with her brother Ray-Ray in California. She used to be so skinny and awkward—not like the way she is now."

Sarah remembered that Dave had spent several

summers in California. When he came home, he always talked about getting into trouble with Ray-Ray Smith. Dave had dozens of funny stories about Ray-Ray's crude practical jokes, but he'd never mentioned Orchid.

Dave glanced at Orchid to make sure she was out of earshot before he went on. "Teri showed up at our doorstep last Friday asking for a place to spend the night. When we called the Smiths' house, they told us all about how she wanted to join Snake Farm. Some boyfriend of hers who was a security guard for a California concert took her backstage to meet the band. Believe it or not, they really did offer her a job." Dave shrugged. "She's always been a little strange. Before Snake Farm, Teri ran away to Hollywood to become an actress. That's when she changed her name to Orchid."

"Then she found out she needed talent and went home," added Sarah.

Dave gave her a surprised look. "Whoa. Where did that come from?"

"Sorry, Dave," Sarah said. "I'm really tired, and I guess it's making me tense."

Dave suddenly bent down and gave her a kiss. "Well, don't be tense about Orchid. You have plenty of competition for my affection," he joked, "but it's not from Orchid."

Sarah gave him a forced smile. Inside she was dying of embarrassment. She hadn't thought she was being that obvious. She looked up into his eyes.

"I wasn't really worried about it," she said.

As Tasha and Sarah left the center, they saw April standing at the pay phone in front of the building. "The line's busy again!" she cried, slamming down the receiver. "My stepmother is talking to one of her stupid friends. How am I supposed to let her know I need a ride?"

Mrs. Gordon gave April a motherly hug and offered to drive her home.

It was nearly 11:30 by the time they climbed into the Volvo. Tasha, Allison, and Sarah piled into the backseat while April got into the passenger's seat.

"I'll drop off the designer and the model at home since it's on the way," Mrs. Gordon told April, gesturing at the backseat. "Then I can take you home."

"Whatever," she replied quietly.

April had lived in more than eight towns before her family had finally settled down in Madison. Her father was a computer salesman, and he was constantly being transferred. April had told Sarah she didn't mind the moving that much, but Sarah wasn't too sure, especially since April's dad had gotten remarried.

"Something wrong, April?" Mrs. Gordon asked. "You're awfully quiet."

"Nothing's wrong," April said with a sigh. "I'm just tired."

Mrs. Gordon didn't press her, but in the backseat Tasha and Sarah exchanged glances.

The lights were on at the Gordon home. Miss Essie came to the door and tried to hug the three drowsy girls at once.

"How did it go?" Miss Essie asked. "I'll bet you were wonderful."

As Tasha and Sarah told her about the show, Mr. Gordon appeared behind Miss Essie with his thumb wrapped in a big roll of gauze and tape.

"Daddy, what happened?" Allison cried.

"Nothing serious. I was just working on those picture frames while I waited for you to come home," he said. "And now look."

"Does it hurt much, Dad?" Sarah asked.

Mr. Gordon pointed the bandaged thumb at Miss Essie. "Not since Florence Nightingale here got through with it. It's not as bad as it looks."

"I don't know how many times I've told my son to be careful around sharp tools," Miss Essie scolded.

"Well, if nobody minds," Tasha said, stifling a yawn, "I'm going to bed. I'm beat."

"Me too," said Sarah, following her cousin's lead.

Mrs. Gordon took the keys out of the front door lock. "I'll be back in fifteen minutes," she said on her way back out to the car. "I still have to take April home . . . oh, you're here!"

No one had heard April get out of the car and cross the yard. She saw Mr. Gordon's injured thumb.

"Oh, Mr. Gordon, that's just awful," she said, bursting into tears.

Tasha and Sarah heard April crying as they were halfway up the stairs. Mr. Gordon looked at them in confusion. Sarah turned and headed back down the stairs, grabbing April in a big hug.

"It's okay," Mrs. Gordon told them. "I'm going to take her home now. Come on, April."

"What was that all about?" Mr. Gordon asked the cousins once Mrs. Gordon had left.

"I don't know. She seemed all right this afternoon," Tasha said.

"Things still aren't right at home then?" Miss Essie said.

The Gordons knew April and Mr. Winter's second wife didn't get along and that was probably what was on April's mind tonight. It didn't help matters that April's stepmother, Alice, was pregnant and Mr. Winter was spending more and more time with her and less and less time with April. Sarah hoped things would get better for their friend soon.

Sarah and Tasha started up the stairs again. "We'll hear all about the Alice vs. April fight tomorrow," said Tasha.

"Count on it," said Sarah. "I hope she'll be okay until then."

At the top of the stairs, the cousins broke into a

run. Tasha reached the bathroom first.

"I'll be right out," she called in a British accent.

Sarah giggled. As she went to her room, she walked past the hall mirror. A big smear of pancake makeup was visible near her neck. Had Dave seen it? she wondered. She stood as tall as she could and made her lips pout the way Orchid's did naturally. Maybe I'm not as tall as she is, she thought to herself, but I'm twice as nice.

She went to her room and waited for Tasha to come out of the bathroom. She knew she was in for a long wait.

Four

Mrs. Parisi quieted the class down as soon as the bell rang. She pulled yesterday's quizzes out of her briefcase and held them in her hand as she sat on a corner of her desk. Her usually friendly face was lined with concern as she tapped the pile of papers on her knee and looked at each student in turn. Tasha squirmed in her seat. She felt a sense of dread.

"I was a little surprised by these quizzes. We talked about the Industrial Revolution for over a week and a half. I have no idea why there were so many poor grades."

Robert Wilson, the class clown, began to hum the suspense music from *Attack of the Killer Zombies*. The class laughed.

"I wouldn't be joking around if I were you, Robert," Mrs. Parisi said sternly. "Your grade was nothing to sing about, unless you know 'Sliding Down Fast.'"

She started distributing the papers and one by one the class members let out groans. Tasha took her paper and flipped it over without looking at the score. Mrs. Parisi gave her a questioning look as she walked past. When the lesson resumed, Tasha's mind was on the quiz on her desk. In several places Mrs. Parisi's red corrections had bled through the paper. While she was getting ready for the fashion show, she'd blown off a lot of her schoolwork. Finally she turned the paper over and braced herself for the blow.

It was a B. Next to the grade, Mrs. Parisi had written, "Not your usual A, what happened?" Tasha put the exam in her notebook and tried to concentrate. It could have been worse, she told herself. Most people would be thrilled with a B. But it wasn't good enough for Tasha. She resolved to do much better on the test next week.

When the bell rang, Mrs. Parisi called Tasha over to her desk.

"I won't keep you long," she said. "I'm guessing that grade you got was a fluke. Your answers in class proved you knew the material. But if you're having some trouble and need more help, I want you to tell me."

"No trouble, Mrs. Parisi," Tasha said. "I'll do better next time."

Her teacher smiled. "I'm sure you will," she responded.

Sarah was waiting for Tasha at her locker. "Guess who's in school today, mate," she said in an English accent.

Tasha rolled her eyes. "What's Orchid doing here? She's too old to be in high school." She twirled the dial on her combination lock and pulled the locker open. She looked in the mirror she had glued to the back of the door as she applied a pale raspberry lipstick.

"I think she's here to meet somebody," Sarah said. She was instantly sorry she had said it. All Billy Turner had talked about at lunch was how hot Orchid had looked last night. By the end of the day every student who had missed the show knew all about the gold lamé bikini and the light blue towel, thanks to Billy.

"If that somebody is Billy, I'm not going to worry about it," Tasha said, shutting her locker firmly. "If that boy can't tell class from trash, he deserves what he gets."

At basketball practice after school, Tasha played hard. She practiced passing the ball with the hand she was dribbling with, never touching it with the other hand. She had seen Michael Jordan do it a hun-

34

dred times, and knew she could get it down. She sent it mostly to Lena Warren, who was always moving toward the basket. After a while, the defender assigned to Tasha just gave up and ran over to double-team Lena. Tasha was worried that the coach would tell her to quit hot-dogging, but she never did.

Tasha remembered that their game against Rector High was coming up. Too bad it's an away game, Tasha thought as her pass found its mark again. The home crowd would eat this stuff up.

At 18 Pine St. Sarah bumped into Kwame as she was going inside. They walked together to their usual booth in the back and discovered that it was already taken—by complete strangers.

A middle-aged couple was sitting there drinking sodas and reading the newspaper. Kwame and Sarah found another table and were checking out the specials on the menu when Cindy joined them. "What happened to our regular table?" she asked.

"Those two were here when we got here," Kwame explained.

Cindy frowned at the couple. "Can't Mr. Harris rope our table off or something? We practically own this place!"

April and Steve Adams were next to join them. Sarah was glad to see the two of them together. It was obvious they liked each other—so far they'd just been slow to do something about it. Sarah expected April to look happy about being there with Steve. Instead her hair was limp and her eyes were bloodshot and dull. She sat down and stared blankly at a spot on the table.

"What's wrong, April?" Sarah asked. "You look terrible."

"I'll be okay, Sarah. I'm just trying to work things out with my dad and stepmother." April sighed. "Don't let me spoil the fun." Steve and Cindy exchanged glances and turned their attention to Kwame, who was pulling a piece of paper from his notebook.

"That's Crispus Attucks," he said, pointing at the photocopied drawing. "He was the first man killed in the Revolutionary War." Kwame ripped the picture out, then he pasted it on a clean sheet of paper.

"Is that for the report you're writing?" Steve asked.

"Uh-huh. Pictures make it more interesting," Kwame said. "Jennifer should check it out—then she might believe these people existed."

The paper began to warp where the glue was. When Kwame tried to smooth it out, he smudged the photocopy. Disgusted, he crumpled it up. "Good thing I made another copy."

"You know," said Steve, "if you scan the picture onto a computer screen and then print it out, you don't have to worry about glue."

Steve was a computer whiz. Sometimes he

showed up at school glassy-eyed after working all night on a program.

Kwame looked at him. "Do you have a scanner?"

Steve nodded. "You're in luck—Steve Adams is on the case. Actually my father is good friends with an architect who has a laser scanner. I helped him hook it up."

"You sure he'll let you?" Kwame said. "I don't want you to get in trouble over this."

"You just get me the books, and tell me which pictures you want. I'll do the rest," Steve reassured him.

April, who hadn't spoken a word, sighed and got up. "I'd better get going," she said.

"But you just got here," Cindy said.

"Yeah," Steve added. "If you want to stay a little longer, I can give you a ride home."

"I'm not in the mood. I don't want to sit in a stupid pizza place all afternoon." She zipped her coat up fast and hoisted her backpack onto her shoulder, nearly hitting Steve with it.

At the door she brushed past Tasha, leaving her friend bewildered.

"What's with April?" Tasha asked the others as she joined them. Before anyone could answer, Mr. Harris came over to the table.

"Have you kids been going to school every day?" he asked.

"Yes." Cindy grinned. "Are you giving out free pizza for perfect attendance?"

"No," Mr. Harris answered. "I just wondered if that man over there who's looking for a Ms. Tasha Gordon is the truant officer."

"He's looking for me?" Tasha said. "What man?"

"That guy sitting over there at your regular table," Mr. Harris said. "He came in here and said he heard that you hung out here. I told him I'd let him know if you came in. You want to talk to him?"

"I guess so," Tasha said. "As long as you don't think he's here to cause trouble."

Mr. Harris went over to where the man was sitting and spoke to him. He nodded in Tasha's direction.

The man got up and approached their table. He was in his fifties or sixties, and had a deep tan. His white hair was long and combed straight back into a ponytail. The woman stayed at the table, smiling at them. Sarah noticed that she was well-dressed and considerably younger than the man.

The man's cologne reached the table before he did. He bowed to the gang and produced a card from the vest of his brown suit. "Hello, everyone," he said with a heavy Dutch accent, "I am Klaus Windmeyer." He set his business card down on the table.

Klaus Windmeyer
President & CEO
Windmeyer, S.A.
The Netherlands

He waited for a response as if he were a famous movie star.

"Hello," Sarah said finally.

Klaus Windmeyer beamed and bowed in Sarah's direction. A fresh cloud of cologne billowed over them all.

"As you can see, I am the president of the Windmeyer Company in the Netherlands," he said. They had to strain to follow his English. "Perhaps you recognize the American products I make. Topper Children's Wear?"

They looked at him blankly.

"Golf Plus Shirts?" he went on. "Avionic Footwear?"

"You're the president of Avionic Shoes?" said Tasha. She had seen the expensive tennis shoes in the athletic store at the mall. "That must be a huge company."

"One of the biggest in the world," he acknowledged enthusiastically. "I am in Madison visiting my brother Hannes. Do you know him? He is a cabinetmaker here." He waved his hand. "But that is not important. My brother took me to your fashion show last night and I was very impressed."

Mr. Windmeyer looked at Tasha. "You are the creator of the Kick-Out Collection?"

Kwame stifled a laugh as Tasha corrected him. Klaus bowed to Tasha.

"That's KickBack, Mr. Windmeyer. The Kick-

Back Collection," Tasha said.

"Kickback?" he said, perplexed.

"Yes. It means relax, be casual," Cindy offered.

Mr. Windmeyer beamed. "Splendid," he cried. "KickBack. As I said I was very impressed by your work. I believe your designs were very inventive. They have the feel of youth." He pronounced it "yute." "And that is why I am here. My firm is committed to expanding its operations in the United States with a line of activewear called Def Soul Casuals. These clothes would appeal to the young man or woman who would like to be . . . eh . . . cool."

A chirping noise suddenly emanated from his pocket. He excused himself with a bow and pulled out a small cellular phone. They got a little relief from his powerful spicy cologne when he stepped away.

"Is this guy for real?" Tasha said in a whisper.

"He sounds legit," Steve murmured.

After a final *ja*, Mr. Windmeyer shut off the phone and lowered the antenna. He turned back to Tasha and the others. "Where were we?" he said.

"Do you want to use the KickBack Collection for your company?" Tasha asked.

Mr. Windmeyer held up a finger. "More than that," he said. "I liked your designs very much, but I need many, many more. And that is why I would like to offer you employment."

Tasha's heart began to beat faster.

"I would like you to design clothing for Def Soul Casuals," Mr. Windmeyer went on. "Def Soul—I think that's a black expression."

"Affirmative on that," Kwame said.

"Wait a minute, Mr. Windmeyer," Tasha said. "You're the president of this company and you want me to design clothes for you?" She wanted to be crystal clear about this—her father had always told her that nothing good comes easy, and this was too easy.

"Right!"

"And you have one of the biggest fashion houses in the world?"

"That is also right," Mr. Windmeyer said.

"Don't you think you should be discussing this with her guardians?" Sarah said.

"Of course!" Mr. Windmeyer cried. "That is the reason I am here now. I want to arrange a meeting with your parents to discuss my offer. But first I wanted to know if you were interested," he said, looking at Tasha.

"I'm very interested," she replied.

"Wonderful. I should think that your parents will be very pleased at this fabulous opportunity."

"My parents are both dead," Tasha said. "I live with my aunt and uncle—you could talk to them."

"I must go back to the Netherlands the day after tomorrow," Mr. Windmeyer said. "If I may, I would like to speak to your aunt and uncle tomorrow. Would that be possible?"

"I think so," Tasha replied eagerly.

"Splendid!" Mr. Windmeyer picked up the business card and wrote his hotel phone number on the back of it with a thick fountain pen. "Please have your aunt or uncle call me to confirm. Now if you please," he said, bowing again, "I must get back to Sonja."

"Way to go, girl," Cindy said when Mr. Windmeyer had gone back to his table.

"Is this really happening to me?" Tasha wondered aloud. She felt dazed.

"I'm a witness if you need one," Steve said.

"Hold on," Sarah said, keeping her voice low. "Nothing's happened yet. We don't know anything about this guy."

Kwame picked up the business card, which still smelled faintly of the man's cologne, and looked at it carefully. "This card could be fake," he said. "You'd better be careful, Tasha."

"Oh, please!" Tasha grabbed the card from Kwame's hand and put it in her pocket. "I think he's legit."

Dave approached their table and pulled up a chair. "Hey, what's up?" He wrinkled his nose. "Did someone drop a bottle of aftershave?" They filled him in on Mr. Windmeyer and his incredible offer. Dave looked over at Mr. Windmeyer, who was talking to his female companion in an animated manner.

"That's great, Tasha. I wish somebody would offer *me* a great job," Dave said.

"Yeah," Kwame chimed in. "How come I never get asked to teach history at Harvard?"

Orchid came over to them and stood behind Dave's chair. Sarah hated to admit it, but Orchid looked great. She wore a bright red blouse with a row of small pearls that formed a V down the front. Her black leather pedal-pushers were a little skimpy for the cold afternoon, but they certainly showed off her long legs.

Orchid tugged on Dave's jacket. "Dave, you promised to take me to the mall today," she whined.

"Yeah, I did." Orchid didn't catch the weary look Dave gave the others.

"I thought you got bored at the mall, Dave," Sarah said.

"I do. I mean, it is boring, sometimes," Dave mumbled.

"Maybe it depends on who you're with," Orchid said, smirking at Sarah.

Orchid toyed with Dave's jacket collar until he got up. He looked annoyed, but he didn't tell her to stop. "Let's go," he said, straightening his collar. "I'll see you all later."

Sarah didn't reply. She was fuming. Cindy grabbed her friend's knee under the table and gave it a sympathetic squeeze. They both could see Tasha's temper rising too.

"One of these days, I just might have to go upside that girl's head," Tasha said.

Mr. Windmeyer approached their table again.

"We are going now. Rest assured, Ms. Gordon, we will have an agreement very soon." He lowered his voice and winked. "By the way, who was that young lady who was standing here not a moment ago?"

Kwame told him.

"I noticed her last night at the fashion show," Mr. Windmeyer said, almost to himself. "Is she a professional model?"

"No, she's a professional musician," said Tasha, barely hiding her disgust.

"Really? How interesting." The businessman bowed once again and left.

At dinner Tasha told Mr. and Mrs. Gordon about Mr. Windmeyer.

Mrs. Gordon had heard of the company. "It's one of the largest European clothing companies," she said. "Their American clothing is very expensive."

"Sounds to me like he's a little crazy," Allison piped up.

"I gotta admit, he sounded crazy, but I think he's just eccentric," said Tasha. "Anyway, we'll find out tomorrow when he comes over. Can I tell him eight o'clock?"

"That's fine," said Mrs. Gordon, looking at Mr.

Gordon, who nodded.

"This could be a big break for me," Tasha mused aloud. "If Mr. Windmeyer likes my designs, I could rise up in his company and become famous!"

"Excuse me, honey," Miss Essie interrupted gently. "As someone in the theater, I'm an authority on big breaks. And I can tell you there aren't any. No matter what you do, you have to pay your dues. You want to work for this man for a while, that's fine. But sooner or later, you'll have to go to design school and learn more about the business."

"He wants to hire me now, not after I finish design school," Tasha said. She couldn't believe that Miss Essie wasn't supporting her. This was the most exciting thing that had ever happened to her. Why was Miss Essie being so negative?

"Fine, girl. I just don't want you to fill your head with unrealistic expectations," Miss Essie said.

"You don't think I've earned my big break, is that it?" Tasha asked.

"Child, I know you haven't," Miss Essie said softly. "But that doesn't mean I'm not pulling for you. I hope this job with Klaus Windmeyer comes through."

"Look, he's an expert," Tasha said. "He should know if I can design or not."

"Your grandmother is just telling you to take things slowly, Tasha," Mrs. Gordon said. "One assignment doesn't automatically means a whole career."

"It sounds to me like she doesn't think I'm talented enough," Tasha said, glaring at Miss Essie. "Mr. Windmeyer could have picked any designer at the show last night, but he chose me because I have the look he wants for his line. Why is that so hard to believe?"

Miss Essie raised her hands. "Forget I said anything. I just wanted to make sure you kept your head on straight, that's all."

After dinner Sarah went upstairs and knocked on Tasha's door. "You all right?" she asked.

"Yeah, thanks. I just want to be alone for a while," Tasha answered.

Sarah shrugged. "Okay," she said. "I'll be around if you want to talk." Sarah was disappointed. She'd been hoping that Tasha needed to talk about how she was feeling—and that she'd have a chance to talk to her about Dave.

Sarah's new relationship with Dave had been off to a great start—she didn't want to see it wrecked by Orchid. She wished she could stop feeling so insecure about Dave. But it was hard, with Orchid around all the time.

Sarah picked up the phone in the hallway and pulled it into her room. She dialed Dave's number and wasn't surprised when Orchid picked up.

"Who's calling, please?" Orchid said.

"Sarah Gordon," Sarah said through clenched teeth.

Orchid didn't answer. The phone was silent for a while, and then Dave came on.

"How was the mall?" Sarah asked.

"Fine," Dave said.

"You weren't bored?"

"Not really, we . . . are you checking up on me?"

Sarah winced. That's exactly what she was doing. "Why, Dave," she said lightly, "should I be?"

"I told you last night there was nothing to worry about."

"I know," said Sarah, "but I haven't seen you much all week and I . . ."

"Well, I've really been busy," Dave said. "There's a dinner for the basketball team coming up and I'm supposed to give a speech. I've been working on it all week and I still only have half of it written."

"If you need to practice it on somebody, I've got some time this weekend." Sarah realized she sounded a little desperate, but she really wanted to see him.

"Sure, okay," Dave responded. "I'll take you up on it."

Sarah suddenly heard Orchid's voice from somewhere in Dave's house. "Davey, come here, quick!" said Orchid.

"Davey! Is that what she calls you?" Sarah asked.

"I guess so . . . she's such a flake," Dave spoke in a whisper. "We're doing Ray-Ray's family a favor by keeping her here. They're hoping she'll change her mind about hooking up with Snake Farm and go home. In the meantime she's driving everyone in my family crazy."

"Including you?"

"I don't know . . . I think . . . maybe, but what difference does it make?"

"Davey!" It was Orchid again.

Dave covered the receiver with his hand, but Sarah could hear him telling Orchid that he was on the phone.

"Where were we?" he said when he got back on.

"You were saying that she was driving you crazy," Sarah said.

"Did I say that?"

Orchid called him again. "Davey, hurry up. I saw a big bug!"

Sarah laughed, breaking the tension a little. "You'd better go."

"No, no. I can talk."

"I don't think she's going to let us," Sarah said.

Dave sighed. "All right. Look, I'll call you back."

Sarah smiled, feeling relieved and much more confident about her and Dave. "Go kill that big bug," she said.

"Don't forget about helping me with my speech," he said before hanging up.

"I won't," she promised. She put the phone back in the hallway and went back to her room. As she lay down on her bed she imagined the scene that was happening between Dave and Orchid. That girl was probably cowering and screaming "Davey!" over a tiny ant or ladybug. Sarah sighed. Orchid certainly knew how to get what she wanted.

Five

"With Tasha's assistance, I think Def Soul Casuals can do very well," Mr. Windmeyer said. He sat on the edge of the Gordons' sofa and smoothed his long white hair with his hand while he waited for Mr. and Mrs. Gordon to respond.

"We think it's very generous of you to offer Tasha a chance to design for your company," said Mrs. Gordon, "but we're her legal guardians and we are more interested in her education. She will have to look for a job soon enough."

"But don't you see?" Windmeyer protested. "I'm not offering her a job, I'm offering her a career."

Come on, Mr. Windmeyer, Tasha urged him in her mind. She sat in the rocking chair quietly listening. She had been anticipating and dreading this moment all day. For a while she had wondered if her meeting with him at 18 Pine St. had been somebody's idea of a practical joke. Would he even show up? Over dinner, she noticed that Mr. and Mrs. Gordon had their doubts too. Tasha caught them trading worried glances when she reminded them of Windmeyer's visit. Then, at precisely eight o'clock, Mr. Windmeyer rang the doorbell, holding a bouquet of flowers for Mrs. Gordon.

Tasha was glad they had the house to themselves. Sarah had gone to Dave's to help him with a speech, and Allison was sleeping over at her best friend Pam's house. Most of all, she was glad Miss Essie was out at a rehearsal. Tasha didn't think Miss Essie would have been impressed by Mr. Windmeyer. At least he didn't stink of cologne the way he had the day before, she noticed with relief.

"The schedule you've described leaves her very little time for school and activities," Mr. Gordon said. "If the Def Soul Casuals line is being launched next fall, that means the order must go to your factories by January. That only gives her a month to work on the designs."

"I can do it!" Tasha blurted. She felt foolish for interrupting them, especially since she had promised she wouldn't. "I can work hard. I can do it."

"And she would be working right here in Madison," Mr. Windmeyer said encouragingly. "When the designs are ready, my company will arrange to

51

have them sent to our American office in New York City."

"If you don't mind a rather blunt question, Mr. Windmeyer," Mrs. Gordon said, "why do you want Tasha to work for you? Why don't you hire a fashion designer with more education and experience in the field?"

Mr. Windmeyer picked up his coffee and sipped it thoughtfully. "An excellent question, and one I'd hoped you would ask," he said. "Mr. and Mrs. Gordon, for a man to make a fortune in my business, he must either be the first or the best. I was very impressed by the freshness of Tasha's imagination. Her ideas are youthful, unique, and unspoiled by years of narrow training. My instincts tell me that Tasha Gordon has a good idea of what people her age would like to wear. Def Soul Casuals will be sold to young men and women very much like Tasha. I have many competitors, as you can imagine, and I believe a clever woman designing a youthful line provides me with an edge."

He picked up another cookie from the tray and washed it down with a swallow of coffee.

"It is true," he continued, "that she'll have to create everything from scratch. And the sketches must be in my New York office by the end of the month. But I do not think it is unreasonable to create twelve sketches of quality in that amount of time."

The room got quiet again. Finally Mrs. Gordon

turned toward Tasha. "Is this how you want to spend your spare time for the next four weeks?" she inquired.

"Yes!" Tasha cried.

"How much would Tasha receive for the work?" Mr. Gordon said.

For the first time that evening, Tasha relaxed. She sensed that the conversation had taken a decisive turn. They were talking money now. Even Mr. Windmeyer looked a little more confident. She hadn't really thought about what she would be paid.

Mr. Windmeyer took a business card out of his pocket and wrote something on the back of it, then handed it to Mr. Gordon. "I think fifteen hundred dollars is fair, don't you?"

Tasha's mind reeled. Fifteen hundred dollars just to draw! She almost blurted out, "I'll take it!", but Mr. Gordon intervened.

"Just a minute," he said. "That comes out to one hundred and twenty-five dollars for every design Tasha provides for you. That's not much for all the labor that's involved for her."

"I'm afraid I didn't make myself clear." Mr. Windmeyer blushed slightly. "I intend to pay fifteen hundred dollars for every design I accept."

Tasha tried to multiply 12 times 1,500, but Mrs. Gordon arrived at the answer first. "You propose to give this child eighteen thousand dollars for a month's work?" said Mrs. Gordon.

"I assure you," said Mr. Windmeyer, "the offer is fair to both myself and Tasha. She will be paid one thousand five hundred dollars for every design that appears in the Def Soul Casuals collection. Even if only one of the pieces becomes a success, my investment will be rewarded."

"Eighteen thousand dollars is a lot of money for a teenager to have," Mr. Gordon said quietly.

"I would not consider her a teenager, but a bright young star in the Windmeyer Corporation. Her official title would be U.S. Representative of the Def Soul line." He produced a manila envelope from his briefcase and handed it to Mrs. Gordon. "Here is a copy of the contract outlining the terms we have just discussed. As a lawyer, I'm sure you'll want to review it."

"Certainly," said Mrs. Gordon briskly.

"Tomorrow I return to my country," he said cheerfully. "I do not want to rush your decision on this matter, but I would like to know your reply by tomorrow morning if possible. I will be in my hotel until ten a.m. After that time, you may fax me at my office in Holland. The number is on my card."

Mr. Windmeyer wiped the crumbs off his lap and stood up. Tasha saw him wink at her, but she was still in shock. Eighteen thousand dollars! She was afraid she would wake up any minute and the dream would be over.

Mr. and Mrs. Gordon showed him to the door.

"I must say," he said as he put his coat on, "this visit to Madison has paid off very handsomely. I never dreamed I would find such high-quality talent in a town this size."

After he left Mr. and Mrs. Gordon went into the den to read the contract. A half hour later, they called Tasha in. Mrs. Gordon had filled two sheets of legal paper with notes. "It looks legitimate," she said finally. They sat Tasha down and closed the door.

All three began talking at once. Tasha was determined to do the work. Her uncle seemed convinced that it was a bad idea, that there would be too much pressure on Tasha and her grades would slip. Finally Mrs. Gordon raised her voice, and Tasha and her uncle looked at her.

"First of all," Mrs. Gordon began, "the contract will *not* be in his hands by ten tomorrow. Business contracts are not my specialty, and I want a colleague of mine to look this over on Monday."

Tasha was crushed. Mrs. Gordon touched her shoulder. "I'm sorry, Tasha, but I have to make sure everything is fair. Besides, I would never counsel a client to sign anything if I wasn't positive she understood it completely."

"But I do!" said Tasha. "I understood what he said here tonight. He said he'd pay me eighteen thousand dollars for twelve sketches."

"Not quite," said Mr. Gordon, pointing at the contract in his wife's hand.

"He will pay you fifteen hundred dollars for every design that makes it all the way to production," said Mrs. Gordon. "He has to approve the sketch, approve the sample, and then test-market the clothes. He can reject it at any point and pay you only a fraction of those fifteen hundred dollars." Mrs. Gordon flipped to the second page of the contract. "If a sketch is initially accepted, and then doesn't make its way through the manufacturing process, you would be paid only one hundred dollars for that sketch."

"That's still twelve hundred dollars," said Tasha.

"If he accepts all twelve sketches," Mr. Gordon reminded her.

"Well, why wouldn't he?" cried Tasha. "He loved my outfits at the fashion show!"

"As long as you understand," Mrs. Gordon said gently.

"What happens if your colleague thinks the contract is okay?" Tasha asked.

"Then you have to make a deal with us," said Mr. Gordon. He wore a no-nonsense expression that made Tasha sit up a little straighter. "You can take Windmeyer's offer if you keep your grades up. If your grades go down, you drop the job. Do you understand?"

"I understand," Tasha assured him.

"Then good luck," said Mrs. Gordon.

Tasha hugged her aunt and uncle and ran up to her

room. Schoolbooks and framed pictures cluttered her desktop. She threw them all on the floor. From under her bed she pulled out a sketchpad and placed it in the center of the desk. She sharpened three pencils and laid them next to the pad. Then she put a pillow on her chair and sat down. Tasha, the world-famous fashion designer, began to draw.

She couldn't wait to tell Sarah!

Six

Sarah walked slowly to Dave's house, savoring the cold air. When she'd left home, Tasha was still waiting for Mr. Windmeyer to arrive. Tasha must be really dedicated to this project, Sarah thought. She'd given up the chance to go out on a Saturday night. Not that Sarah wouldn't do the same thing. It was an incredible opportunity.

Sarah could smell wood smoke from a fireplace; it was a perfect night for it. The lights at Dave's house looked warm and beckoning as they cast their glow over the frost-covered grass.

Dave answered the door wearing cutoff jeans and a tank top with the number 23 on it.

"Some date, huh?" he joked. "I ask a girl over to help me with a speech."

"I don't mind. Want to take a walk before we get started?"

Dave's smile faded. "Love to," he said, "but I'm all alone in the house and I'm supposed to wait for my father's boss to call."

"Must be pretty important if he's calling on a Saturday night."

"It better be," Dave grumbled. "I wasn't born to be an answering machine. My dad says we don't need a machine—that's because *he* never has to stay home and wait for the phone."

Sarah followed him into the kitchen. He filled two glasses of orange juice and handed one to her.

"Where's Orchid?" Sarah asked casually.

"At the mall, as usual. I think she should have her mail sent there," Dave said.

"I'm surprised she didn't insist on dragging you along."

"Don't think she didn't try," said Dave. "I swear that girl has only one thing on her mind."

"Sex?" Sarah ventured.

"No, Orchid!" They both laughed. "You know what?" he said. "All of a sudden I don't mind being stuck here." He smiled at her, then finished his juice and ran some water into the glass. "Come upstairs, I want to show you something."

She followed him to the second floor, taking two steps at a time while he took three.

They passed the room Orchid was using. It was

almost across the hall from Dave's. Through the partly opened door Sarah saw dozens of brand-new clothes tossed all over the floor. Many still had price tags on them. A vanity table was covered with rows of brightly colored lipsticks and eyeshadows. A bright blue wig hung from the back of a chair.

On her dresser mirror Orchid had taped a picture of the lead singer in Snake Farm. He was a short, muscular man with muttonchop whiskers and long stringy red hair.

"In here," Dave called from his room. Sarah walked in as he rummaged through his desk. His room was just as cluttered as Orchid's, but with basketball shoes, towels, and books. A dozen basketball trophies stood on a shelf; some were small figurines, others stood nearly three feet tall with gold and silver columns and walnut pedestals. A basket of neatly folded laundry sat by the dresser.

"Here it is," Dave said triumphantly. He handed Sarah a letter.

Dear Mr. Hunter:

Congratulations! You have been selected from an outstanding field of high school students to attend Polytechnic University on a full athletic scholarship. This is contingent upon your successful completion of your high school curriculum . . .

Sarah finished reading it and looked up. "That's wonderful, Dave," she said. "Now you have Polytechnic and Stanford fighting over you, and you're not even a senior yet!"

Dave looked pleased. "It's great," he said, folding the letter. "Of course, I don't plan to go there, but at least it's another choice. I can't wait to hear from some of the big state schools."

He glanced at his watch. "I'd better get to work on that speech," he said. He picked up a notebook and a pen from the foot of his bed. "I know what I want to say, but it's not coming out right."

"Try out what you have on me," Sarah said. She pushed some clothes off a blue beanbag chair and settled in.

Dave read what he had written as Sarah listened carefully, stopping him now and then to clear up a phrase or two. They worked on the speech for almost an hour, taking a break for sodas and pretzels.

At 9:15, they heard the rattle of the lock and the front door opening. "If that's my dad, then I'm free to take that walk with you," said Dave.

"Anybody home?" Orchid shouted from the hallway.

Dave looked at Sarah and shrugged. Sarah muffled her laughter as Dave yelled back that he was home and that he was busy.

Sarah could hear Orchid climbing the stairs slowly,

her shopping bags rustling with every step. "I'm glad you're here, Davey," she called out in a girlish voice, "I want to see what you think of this gorgeous camisole I . . ." Her words faded away when she reached Dave's doorway and saw Sarah in the room.

"Hi, Orchid," said Sarah pleasantly. She had noticed with satisfaction that Orchid had spoken without a British accent all the way up the stairs.

"Hello," Orchid replied flatly. She turned to Dave with a disapproving look. "Davey, why didn't you tell me you had a girl up in your room?" She cocked an eyebrow and then whirled around and headed for her room.

Sarah immediately stood up from the beanbag chair. She knew Orchid was trying to imply that she'd just walked in on a big love scene. But she was dead wrong.

"Don't let her get to you," Dave whispered.

"I'm trying not to, Dave," Sarah answered between gritted teeth. "It's just that she's the one . . ."

Orchid suddenly reappeared at the door. She had taken off her camel's hair jacket and her suede ankle-high boots. Now she wore green wool hunting pants that had been tailored for her slim form, and a red checked shirt. Dave scowled at Orchid.

"How did you get back from the mall anyway?" he demanded.

"Oh, I got a ride," said Orchid brightly, sticking her thumb out.

Hitchhiking! Sarah was amazed. Orchid might be beautiful, but she acted pretty stupid.

"You were supposed to get picked up by my mother at nine-thirty," Dave reminded her in an angry tone. "Now she's going to drive all the way to the mall for nothing."

"I got bored," Orchid commented. She raked her short hair with her fingers. "Lighten up."

Dave got up and brushed past her to call his mother at her choir practice.

While Dave was gone, Orchid came into his room. Sarah watched as she picked up a clean shirt from the laundry basket and put it in his drawer. She straightened the bedspread he had been lying on. "Dave can be so messy," she said, smiling. "But he's so cute. Especially in the morning."

"Yeah, well, I wouldn't know about that," said Sarah.

"No, I guess you wouldn't," Orchid said sweetly.

Sarah made her way to the bedroom door. She was determined not to let Orchid make her lose her temper, but that didn't mean she had to stand around watching her straighten Dave's room. Something about the way she did it made Sarah feel it wasn't the first time.

"Davey is mad because I came back early and caught him with you," said Orchid, closing Dave's notebook and placing it neatly on his desk. "But I've told him a million times, it doesn't bother me if he wants to see other girls. I want an open relationship."

Sarah felt her heart starting to pound. "Other girls? What are you talking about?" she said hotly. "Dave doesn't even like you."

"Is that what he told you?" Orchid said, looking at Sarah with pity. "You know how men are." Orchid stretched out on Dave's bed and fixed her large green eyes on Sarah.

Sarah gave Orchid a look of contempt.

Orchid didn't seem to notice. She lifted her head from the bed and pulled a corner of the bedspread down. Then she ran her hand under Dave's pillow and came out with a large photograph.

"Do you like this picture of me? I think it makes me look fat. What do you think?" She held up the color picture. She was posed with her hands behind her back, her chest and hips jutting forward. She wore a black bra and tight black bicycle pants—nothing else.

Sarah stared at the photo in shock. For a few seconds she couldn't move or say a word.

"I hope you're happy, Orchid," Dave yelled upstairs. "Mom's already left to pick you up."

The phone rang once and through her fog Sarah heard Dave pick it up and say hello.

Sarah forced herself to move. She walked woodenly down the stairs and removed her coat from the closet. As she opened the front door, she glanced in the living room. Several old photographs rested on top of Mrs. Hunter's piano. One of Orchid had been added to the collection.

Sarah slammed the door behind her.

She walked around the block twice before she stopped crying. In her mind she kept seeing Orchid's flashy bicycle pants and black bra. She didn't know what was more upsetting—Dave's being attracted to a girl like that, or the fact that he had lied to her about it.

Tasha's door was closed, but Sarah had to tell somebody. She knocked once, then walked into the room.

"Tasha, I—"

"I got the job!" shrieked Tasha. Sarah saw a pile of crumpled sheets of paper scattered around her chair. A half dozen color markers lay on top of the sketchpad.

"That's wonderful, Tasha." Sarah forced herself to smile.

Tasha told her about Windmeyer's visit, and how she had one month to come up with twelve pieces for the Def Soul collection.

"I could get as much as eighteen thousand dollars! Can you believe it?"

Sarah tried to listen, but her heart wasn't in it. Tasha was too excited with her own news to notice that anything was wrong.

"I'll let you get back to your sketches," said Sarah,

feigning enthusiasm. As she closed her cousin's door, Sarah felt lonelier than ever. Tasha had every right to be excited, but what about Sarah's problems?

She poked her head in her parents' bedroom. Mrs. Gordon was putting on her coat.

"Can we talk a little later, honey?" her mother said. "Your father and I are going to a late movie."

Miss Essie's light was on and her door was ajar. Sarah knocked softly, then tiptoed away when there was no answer. Her grandmother had probably fallen asleep while she was reading.

"You have to give an old girl a little time," Miss Essie said, appearing at the door. She motioned for Sarah to come in.

Miss Essie's room was small, but in perfect order. Nearly every empty space on the wall was covered with photos, posters, and framed newspaper clippings of plays such as *Love in the Air* and *Blues Night Special* that she had appeared in. Miss Essie closed the script she was reading and motioned Sarah to the only chair in the room, while she lay on her bed.

"You look awful, child," said Miss Essie bluntly.

"I feel awful," said Sarah, a sob creeping into her throat.

Miss Essie nodded now and then as Sarah told her about Dave Hunter and Teri Smith, alias Orchid.

"I know I shouldn't feel so bad—I mean, we're not engaged or anything. It just hurts that he lied

66

about it." Sarah looked away as fresh tears welled in her eyes. "He kept telling me how boring she was, and I think he meant it. He's just attracted to her body. I can't compete with that."

"Are you sure you're reading Dave right?" Miss Essie said.

"She pulled her picture out from under his pillow! What am I supposed to think?" Sarah said.

"Don't sell yourself short, girl," Miss Essie said. "You're a very beautiful young woman. And if Dave is the boy I think he is, he won't waste too much time on this Orchid girl. But if he does, that's something you should be glad to know about him." Miss Essie looked around at the framed playbills on her wall until she found one for a play called *Shout About It!*

"Did I ever tell you about Amos Coulter?" Miss Essie said, pointing at the playbill. "His friends used to call him A.C. What happened with me and Amos reminds me of you and Dave. We were in that play together, and I was in love with that man. A.C. played the part of a small-town preacher. He was handsome and burly with a voice like a trumpet. Best part was, he liked me too. We used to talk for hours and never run out of things to say."

"What happened?" said Sarah.

"Dorothy Davis happened," her grandmother said sourly. "She was one of the chorus girls and she was a gorgeous little so-and-so. Couldn't act to save her life, mind you, but that didn't matter. Like I said,

A.C. liked me very much, but this other girl was red-hot. She had a reputation as a man-eater. Do you know how bad you had to be to get a reputation in the theater at that time?" Miss Essie laughed.

"That Dorothy turned his head all the way around. He started breaking dates with me and acting different. Your grandmother is no fool; I saw what was what and I told him, 'A.C., you got a choice between sexy and stupid, which is what she is, and beautiful and smart, which is what I am.' "

"And?"

"And he went for sexy and stupid."

"They all go for sexy and stupid!" Sarah wailed.

"Really? What about your father?" Miss Essie asked.

She had Sarah there. "So what did you do about A.C.?" she asked.

"I won't lie to you." Miss Essie's expression got thoughtful. "It hurt my pride for a loooong time. And it's going to hurt you a long time too. After a few weeks of moping around, a good friend of mine sat me down and said, 'Essie, a man who can't appreciate you isn't worth hurting about.' "

Sarah thought about that for a second, then stood up. She gritted her teeth and repeated, "A man who can't appreciate me isn't worth hurting about."

Miss Essie's eyes sparkled. "Your grandfather had a way with words."

PINE

Seven

On Sunday, after the Gordon family returned from church, Mr. Gordon announced that he was taking them all to the Sea Cove for brunch.

"You all go." Tasha shook her head. "I have to stay and work."

"I thought we could celebrate your new job," Mr. Gordon said. "How are the designs coming?"

"Not bad," Tasha said brightly.

The truth was, she was a little nervous. The night before she had planned to whip off at least fifteen sketches, then pick the best. But every outfit she sketched looked like something she had seen in a magazine. It has to be totally different, she told herself as she crumpled sheet after sheet. It had to be a

Tasha Gordon Original. Four hours later she had crawled into bed, telling herself to relax, it was only the first day.

As the rest of the family piled into the car and headed for the Sea Cove, Sarah thought about Tasha. Usually her cousin could juggle ten activities at once and excel in each of them. This time, though, Tasha seemed to be struggling. Sarah hoped that Tasha hadn't made a mistake in taking this job.

After brunch Sarah walked the three blocks to the Westcove Mall and waited for Cindy by the doors under the Ms. Tique sign.

Cindy appeared wearing a colorful heavy shawl. "It's from the Islands," she said proudly. "It's too strange to wear to school, but here . . . Hey—" She looked at Sarah closely—" where were you last night? It doesn't look like you got much sleep."

Sarah was thrilled to have someone actually notice that she was down. She poured her heart out to Cindy, who listened closely. Then Sarah's friend wrinkled her nose in disgust. "Men are dogs," she said flatly. "If Dave acts like that, they *all* act like that."

They walked to the food court for sodas and spied April sitting alone, with several crumpled napkins strewn around the table.

"You thought *you* had troubles," Cindy murmured to Sarah. She quickly explained that April had shown up at Jennifer's door last night holding a suitcase. "She left home and figured that Jennifer and her mom had plenty of room in that big house. Jennifer was dying to know why she ran away, but April wouldn't say anything to her."

Now Sarah was really concerned about their friend. She hadn't been herself for days. "Hey, April, are you all right?" she said as they approached.

"What do you care!" snarled April.

Sarah kept her voice level. "Whatever it is, April, you have to tell somebody. It doesn't have to be us, but you've got to let it out. You look terrible!"

April looked at them, tears welling in her eyes. "You wouldn't look so good either if your family was falling apart!"

She told her friends about the fight she had had with Alice and her father the night before. "They were screaming horrible things at each other. In the middle of the fight, my dad just walked to the door and said he had to go. Then I started screaming at Alice. I told her she was driving my father crazy. She said *I* was driving *both* of them crazy. She made it sound like their fight was my fault. I . . . I didn't think my dad was going to come back."

"Just because your parents had a fight, your father isn't going to abandon you," Cindy pointed out. "People who love each other sometimes fight. It's a fact."

"You don't know my father," April said hoarsely. "I mean . . . I love him, but he's afraid of responsibility. Look at what happened with him and my real mother. They were fine until I came along, then the pressure became too much. It's going to get worse when Alice has her baby."

Sarah and Cindy looked at each other. They didn't know what to say, so they kept silent and listened. April also confessed she was afraid her father would love the child he had with Alice more than her. "That baby will be *their* baby together. I'm just the product of a previous mistake," she said.

"Do they know how you feel about all this?" said Sarah.

"I can't talk to them about it." April gave her friends a sad smile. "But I'm glad you let me get it out."

Suddenly Cindy and Sarah had the same idea. They each grabbed one of April's arms and hoisted her up. "You're coming with us," Cindy said.

They took her to the Hairport first, and despite April's protests, paid for a haircut and blow-dry. Then they attacked the makeup counter of Worth's Department Store, where they told April to get a shade of nail polish that matched her blue sweater. Outside the store they sat on a bench and April watched in silence as Cindy painted the unusual color on her fingernails. At least she's letting us do this, Sarah thought. It's bound to cheer her up a little.

When the nail polish dried, Cindy and Sarah surveyed April critically. Her hair was back to its shiny golden color. Her face was back to pink, not red. But her eyes were still distant and sad.

"How do you feel?" Sarah asked her.

"Better, I guess," April admitted. "You let me forget for a little while."

As they walked through the mall, Jennifer approached them with a murderous look in her eye.

"I'll kill her!" she hissed. "Remember that little red miniskirt at Ms. Tique? The one in the window? Somebody bought it! I'll bet my mother's credit card it was Orchid."

"Anybody could have bought that skirt," Cindy said.

"Trust me, it was her," Jennifer said hotly. "I saw her looking at it the other day. It's just the kind of thing she'd wear, don't you think?"

Sarah had to agree.

"I'll bet they have more than one," said Cindy. "Go back to the store and ask them."

Jennifer exhaled impatiently. "And be the second person in Madison with the same skirt? That's no fun." She looked at Cindy, Sarah, and April and added gravely, "This is turning out to be the worst day!"

April, remembering her own troubles, began to laugh. Cindy stifled a giggle. As Jennifer looked from one to the other, Sarah, too, began to laugh. Leave it to Jennifer, with her obsession with shopping, to be the one who finally made April laugh.

Tasha got up from her desk and began combing her hair in front of the bathroom mirror. She was so frustrated she wanted to scream. She felt like she wasn't getting anywhere with these stupid sketches.

It was a huge relief when Sarah dashed up the stairs. "Any luck with the designs?" she called out.

"No," Tasha said. "How was the mall?"

Sarah told her about April and Jennifer. Tasha smiled. "Maybe I should have gone. I think I need to see some clothes to inspire me."

"Why don't you open that closet of yours," Sarah teased. Tasha wasn't as crazy about clothes as Jennifer was, but she still had plenty. "If you need any help, let me know."

Tasha thanked her and sat at her desk again. Her back ached from leaning over the sketchpad. She shook her fingers, which were starting to cramp when she gripped the pencil. She heard Sarah going into her bedroom. The faint music from her radio reached Tasha through the open door. She was tempted to call Sarah back so that they could shoot ideas back and forth. They used that system when they were planning a party or a school event. Then she remembered that it had to be a Tasha Original.

Tasha put the pencil down and leaned back in her chair and closed her eyes. She tried to bring back her fantasy about living like a designer. But every time she saw herself boarding a plane, or drinking champagne on a yacht, her mind flashed to the drawing table and her cramped fingers. "This has got to get easier," she told herself.

With a jolt she remembered Mrs. Parisi's history test coming up this week. She also remembered her uncle's statement: "You must keep your grades up; that's all I ask." She let out a loud groan and put the sketchpad away. She rummaged in her bookbag for the textbook, then realized with numb dread that she had left it in her locker. "Get a grip!" she chided herself. She tried to work on her math homework instead, but her attention kept wandering. How was she ever going to pull this off?

Tasha picked up a sheet of paper and wrote down her activities. Classes came first, of course, then basketball, homework, dinner, sleep. She looked at the blank spaces that were left. A few hours were scattered throughout the week and the weekends. "I have three more weekends," she reminded herself. Creating four designs a week shouldn't be a problem. Her eye fell on the crumpled balls of paper at her feet. At this rate she was going to lose the designing job as fast as she'd gotten it. Maybe Miss Essie was right; she just hadn't paid her dues. The problem was, Tasha wasn't sure she'd be able to live up to the promise she'd made to Uncle Donald either.

Eight

The lunch menu at Murphy High was printed on a large board: chicken and rice, Tater Tots, green beans, fruit juice, and pudding. After Steve gave Kwame his potatoes in exchange for Kwame's green beans, he pulled a folder out of his backpack. He showed Kwame the scanned drawings he'd created for Kwame's report.

"Awesome." Kwame rubbed his finger lightly over the drawing. "It really looks professional."

"That's nothing," Steve said proudly. "At first I had some trouble using the scanner, but I fiddled with the commands for a while, and it came out all right."

José sat down with them and picked up one of the drawings.

"Careful with those," Steve warned. "I don't think I'll be able to use the system again."

"It would have been just as easy to cut the picture out of a photocopy, then paste it on a blank sheet," José said.

"Sure," said Steve, not masking his disdain. "While we're at it, let's go back to living in caves."

Shouts from the table where the jocks sat distracted them. The jocks were yelling at a hall monitor who was trying to stop Orchid from coming into the cafeteria. Orchid was pleading with the monitor and pointing to Billy Turner. Finally, the monitor gave up and Orchid burst into the room. Nearly every head turned.

She had on a red leather miniskirt, a pair of pink tights, and a small red leather jacket with big silver studs. The whoops and whistles reminded Kwame of the fashion show. Orchid smiled at Billy, and then sat down with him and the rest of the football team.

"Wow," said José, turning back to his food. "She is hot."

"If you like the type." Kwame shrugged.

"What are you talking about, Kwame?" Steve said. "She's perfect! You wouldn't go out with her if you could?"

Kwame looked uncomfortable. "She's gorgeous, but I don't think we have anything in common."

"Don't worry about that," José said. "The last

thing a guy wants to do with a girl like Orchid is *talk*."

Tasha waited inside the main office of Murphy High to see one of the guidance counselors. She had just left history class and the test which she knew she had failed. More than half the questions had been on the chapter Mrs. Parisi had assigned for the weekend. As the clock had raced toward the dismissal bell, Tasha had bluffed her way through a few essay questions and guessed on most of the multiple choice. She had never been so irresponsible about schoolwork before. The reality of her history test had made Tasha realize how behind she was in all of her classes. But, Tasha reminded herself, you've never been a working fashion designer before.

Tasha had remembered hearing about a senior who had to work after school every day. Her guidance counselor had talked to her teachers. They'd agreed to give her extensions on homework and some tests. Surely Tasha's teachers would appreciate the pressure she was under from basketball and fashion designing, and would allow her some extra time.

Mr. Leffert's door swung open and a heavyset girl walked out. He motioned Tasha inside. His office had a full-length window, but he had the blinds shut. His desk was off to one side. On the wall behind his desk he had several wooden paddles with students' names burned in them.

"They're just novelties," Mr. Leffert assured her when he caught her staring at them. He was a tall man with a crew cut and a big bushy beard. His gray suit looked brand-new, but his shirt was yellowed and frayed at the collar.

"Congratulations, Tasha. It's all over the school that you've been offered a job. I think that's wonderful."

Tasha thanked him. Her friends from 18 Pine had been the first to find out and they had spread the news quickly. After her first class today she had returned to a locker full of handwritten notes: "Congratulations!" "Don't forget us little people on your way to the top." People had been patting her shoulder and shaking her hand all morning. Even so, she was surprised that Mr. Leffert had found out.

"What can I do for you today?" Mr. Leffert said, leaning back so that his chair tipped against the wall.

"I wanted to talk to you about my classes," Tasha started.

"You don't think you're getting enough homework?" Mr. Leffert said, laughing.

"Get serious," Tasha was tempted to say. Instead, she politely explained the work Mr. Windmeyer had asked for. "I was wondering if I could get some extensions on my schoolwork this month," she went on.

Mr. Leffert laughed again. His chair squeaked as he brought it forward. "I don't think that's possible," he said.

"I heard there was a senior who had a job after school and you worked out things for her," Tasha said indignantly. "I'm just asking for the same break."

"Not that it's any of your business, but that girl is trying to finish school and take care of her mother and her sister," he said. He leaned back in his chair again. "If you're feeling pressed for time, I'd suggest cutting back on your extracurricular activities."

"Like the basketball team?" Tasha asked.

"That's a start. How would it look if I went around to all your teachers and said, 'Can Tasha Gordon have an extension on her work so she can work on her designs after basketball practice?' " Mr. Leffert shook his head. "No can do."

"Is it possible to take some time off from school?" Tasha asked. "You know, like get a leave of absence or something?"

Mr. Leffert leaned forward and brought the chair down hard. "That's the last thing you should consider," he said sternly. "School should be your first priority."

"I could make up the work over Christmas vacation," Tasha said quickly.

Mr. Leffert shook his head. "Tasha . . . look, you want to handle a lot of things, and you're capable of handling a lot of things, I'm sure," he said. "But you're also old enough to know what's most important."

"I know education is important," Tasha insisted. "But it's mostly important because it helps you get a job—and now I have one."

Mr. Leffert's brow furrowed. "I just don't want you to throw away all your choices. The fact is that the more education you have, the more choices you're going to have for the rest of your life."

"Why can't you see that my choice is keeping this job with Mr. Windmeyer?" Tasha could feel the tears stinging her eyes. "If school is about choices, then I know what choice I want to make—I'll quit school!"

"What I'm saying, Tasha, is that you're dealing with one choice now. And it's a choice you might well regret later on. What if the job with Windmeyer doesn't pan out? Then where will you be?"

"All I know is, if I don't have more time to work on those designs, I won't *have* a job with Mr. Windmeyer." Tasha got up to leave.

Mr. Leffert picked up the phone. "Stay there," he ordered. "We're going to discuss this with the principal."

But Tasha ran out of the office. Mr. Leffert hung up and strode after her, but she was gone.

Sarah and Tasha were surprised to see both Mr. and Mrs. Gordon waiting for them when they got home from 18 Pine St. Mr. Gordon looked concerned. He motioned for Tasha to sit down.

"What did your colleague say about Mr. Windmeyer's contract?" Tasha eagerly asked Mrs. Gordon.

"He said it's unusual, but it's legitimate. Tasha, we got a call from your guidance counselor. Is it true you're thinking of quitting school?"

"No, not really," said Tasha, thinking about her ordeal with Mr. Leffert. "I just need more time to work on the designs."

Mrs. Gordon put a hand on Tasha's knee. "Baby, your uncle and I are happy that you got this job, but we're worried that it will take up too much of your time. Quitting high school is simply not an option."

"I told you, I didn't mean it. But even if I did quit, I could always take the GED."

"Tasha, the General Equivalency Degree is not for someone like you," said Mr. Gordon. "It's for people who are too old to attend high school, or someone who's in jail and has no other choice. You could take the GED right now and pass it. You have to finish high school so you can go on to college as you planned before Windmeyer came along."

"Mr. Windmeyer doesn't need a person with all that education. He needs someone fresh," said Tasha.

As Sarah listened, she could see both sides. This truly was a great opportunity for Tasha, but it was upsetting to hear her talking about quitting school.

"What happens a few years from now when you're not so fresh?" said Mrs. Gordon. "You'll be in your twenties, praying you'll find a job that won't ask you for a college diploma."

The telephone rang and Tasha ran over to pick it up before her aunt and uncle could stop her. She heard a crackly long-distance hiss, then Mr. Windmeyer's voice.

"*Ja*, is this Ms. Tasha Gordon?"

"Yes, it is." What timing! Tasha thought.

"How are you? Are you sketching out the future of clothing in America?"

"Trying to," she said.

"That's good news," Mr. Windmeyer said. "Because I have been able to move our production schedule up by almost a week. With your help we will be able to destroy the competition. Do you think you can send the sketches to me in three weeks?"

"I'll certainly try," Tasha said, trying to sound confident.

"A try doesn't sell. A try doesn't make you famous," Windmeyer said. "Please send my warmest regards to your family." He hung up.

"That was Mr. Windmeyer," Tasha said. She explained what he wanted.

"That doesn't give you much time at all," Mrs. Gordon said. "And you were already feeling pressured."

"It's only twelve sketches," Tasha said. "I can do it."

"A minute ago, four weeks was too hard," Mr.

Gordon said. "How are you going to handle this?"

"I'm old enough to figure this out on my own." Tasha ran to her room and slammed the door.

Sarah went upstairs and knocked softly on Tasha's door. She expected Tasha to be crying on her bed after an outburst like that. Instead she had her back to the door, and she was working on the designs at her desk. She had taped fashion spreads from *Young & Sassy* on the wall in front of her for inspiration.

"Hey, cuz, what's happening?" Sarah asked.

"It's certainly not me," Tasha said. "And it's certainly not these designs."

"Do you think Dad could be right?" Sarah asked gingerly. "It does seem like you're under pressure."

Tasha turned to face her. "To tell you the truth, I know he's right. But I know what I want right now—and I'll do whatever it takes to get it!"

Sarah believed her. Tasha could be very stubborn when her mind was made up.

"Hey, girl, you go for it," Sarah said. "I've got your back."

Tasha grinned and gave her a thumbs up. "Thanks."

At dinner the Gordons avoided the topic of fashion designing. Instead they listened to Miss Essie describe her day.

"I did a voice-over audition for a radio commercial today," Miss Essie announced. "I had to say 'Denturite is all right' at least a hundred different

84

ways. Anybody who thinks acting is glamorous is a fool. How's your thumb, son?"

"Fine," said Mr. Gordon. He moved it slowly back and forth. "You did a great bandaging job."

"I played a nurse once and I thought I would be more convincing if I learned basic first aid. It pays to do some research."

"I'm glad you never had to play a bank robber!" said Mr. Gordon with a wink.

Everybody laughed except Tasha. A few minutes later, when she asked to be excused from the table, Mrs. Gordon nodded. No one said a word as they watched her put her coat on and step outside.

The park was well lit, but Tasha stayed on a path close to the street just to be safe. She stepped carefully on the gravelly road so that her shoes wouldn't cake up with mud. The trees were bare, and the city behind them looked like it was trapped in the branches. Tasha stared at the lovely, mysterious effect for a minute, then whipped out a pencil and a slip of paper and tried to capture it. The pattern would look dramatic on a fall jacket. It was thrilling to actually be creating something again.

She didn't know how long she'd been crouching there, when she noticed a pair of feet in front of her. She looked up at Mr. Gordon.

"Mind if I sit with you?" he said.

Tasha shook her head. "You know," she blurted out. "My mother didn't go to college at all."

Mr. Gordon looked surprised by her comment. "Things have changed since then, Tasha," he said.

"Not enough," Tasha replied ruefully. "There are still better opportunities for men than for women. Sometimes I don't think the world is a very fair place."

"Me too," Mr. Gordon acknowledged. "But things have gotten better. I guess that's one reason I'm opposed to your even thinking of leaving school. There are a lot of opportunities out there. I don't want you to explore only one of them."

"But Uncle Donald, this job could turn into a real career," Tasha insisted.

"That's certainly possible," Mr. Gordon admitted. "But do you want to bet the rest of your life on that possibility?"

Tasha shrugged.

Mr. Gordon was silent for a moment. "Your mother and I talked about education several times," he said. "She told me that because she was a woman—a black woman—she felt she had to take the first job she could get. An education seemed like a luxury. After she married your dad, they did all right. But she always vowed that her daughter would have a better education than she did. That her daughter would never be afraid for her future."

"Mom used to ask Dad what kind of future he thought he would have, after he retired from playing ball," Tasha admitted. "I think he was afraid to talk about it."

"Do you think they would want their daughter to have that fear?" Mr. Gordon said.

Tasha looked at him, tears brimming in her eyes. "I don't know," she said. "I don't know anymore."

Mr. Gordon took a handkerchief out of his pocket and gave it to Tasha. Tasha wiped her eyes, thinking of her parents. What would they want her to do now? Sometimes it was so hard to be without them. Would she ever stop missing them so terribly?

Her uncle gave her a big hug. She hugged him back, crying softly on his shoulder.

18
PINE

Nine

By the next morning Tasha had decided that quitting school wasn't really an option—at least not until she knew more about her future with Mr. Windmeyer. So she'd have to scale back on basketball for at least a few days. She dreaded telling the coach that she needed a few days off.

The big game against Rector was coming up on Thursday night, and team needed her. The coach might even kick her off the team.

Tasha took a deep breath as she entered the girls' locker room. "What is it, Gordon?" Mrs. Keiser spoke without looking up from her desk.

"I can't make it to practice this afternoon, Coach."

Mrs. Keiser raised her head slowly. "I see," she said.

"And I'm not going to be able to make tomorrow night's game either."

"You got the game schedule early in the year. You didn't mention you had any conflicts." The coach spoke slowly.

"Something came up," Tasha said. Mrs. Keiser was making it hard on her. Tasha wished the coach would get mad at her, but she merely kept writing.

"Aren't you going to ask me why?" Tasha asked.

"I can't worry about that," Mrs. Keiser said. "You told me you can't make practice, and you won't be at the game tomorrow. Fine. It doesn't really matter why, does it?"

"No, but . . ." Tasha wanted to explain that she just needed a little time, that a great opportunity had come up, but the coach didn't want to hear it. Oh well, Tasha told herself as she walked away. I guess making choices is part of the price of success.

Sarah bumped into Dave as he walked out of English class. His eyes lit up when he saw her. He quickly guided her over to the side of the corridor, away from the mob of students.

"How've you been?" he asked.

"Fine. *Where* have you been?" she responded coldly.

"I've been busy these days," he said vaguely, but his eyes were still warm and focused on her.

89

"Busy with somebody else?"

Dave looked away and shifted his feet. Finally he looked at her again.

"Look," he said, "we have to talk about what happened the other day at my house. I think you misunderstood what was going on, and I can see how you could."

Sarah hoped he was right. She wanted him to say that Orchid had put the picture in his bed.

"Anyway," he continued, "I want to talk to you about it in a less public place." He gestured at the crowded hallway, noisy with the sound of slamming lockers.

"Great. How about tonight?"

Dave bit his lip. "I can't tonight. I was thinking about sometime tomorrow."

"I don't know," Sarah said cautiously, "I'm pretty busy sometime tomorrow."

"Are you bugging out on me again?" Dave said exasperatedly.

"Why not tonight? Is it because of Orchid?"

"Tonight?" Dave looked flustered. "It's just that . . . well, I mean . . . My mom's having a dinner party and so Orchid wanted me to take her out for Chinese food tonight and —"

Sarah didn't wait for Dave to finish what he was saying. She just stormed off.

"And since you don't believe me," he yelled after her, "I might as well have something going with her.

At least you'd have a reason to be acting like you are."

Sarah didn't turn around. She concentrated on Miss Essie's words. "He's not worth hurting about."

Later that evening, Sarah noticed the group of cars parked in front of Dave's house. Dave and Orchid must have been back from dinner by now, she fumed to herself, and he was probably showing her off to his mother's guests!

Sarah glanced at herself in the hall mirror. She had never thought of herself as plain before Orchid arrived. Maybe she wasn't as glamorous as Tasha, or as stylish as Jennifer, but she had felt confident about her looks. Now Orchid's green eyes and slinky body made Sarah feel totally unappealing. How could Dave possible resist someone like Orchid? It wasn't his fault that he found the girl so attractive, she decided. Suddenly Sarah was determined to win Dave back—even if she had to fight for him.

She ran a finger across her eyelid as if she were spreading a garish slash of eyeliner on it. She touched her cheeks and imagined the skin with a brown-red undertone to it. Then she brushed her fingertip to her lips as an idea gathered energy in her mind.

While Tasha was in the bathroom, Sarah went into her room and borrowed the slinkiest tank top and the tightest jeans Tasha owned. Then she took some makeup from Tasha's top drawer and ran to her room.

I can't be stupid and sexy, she thought. But maybe I can be smart and sexy!

Ten

The gathering at the Hunters' house was coming to an end by the time Sarah rang the doorbell. Mrs. Hunter opened it and the smile froze on her face. She had never seen Sarah with black eyeliner and bright green eyeshadow.

"Come in, Sarah," she said finally. Sarah felt a little embarrassed waiting in the hallway while Mrs. Hunter went to look for Dave. Maybe she'd overdone it a little. The Hunters' guests were openly staring at her. At least she had on her jacket.

Dave appeared, wearing black pants and a new sweater. He looked a little startled at all the makeup Sarah had on, but he didn't say anything. He led her to the kitchen.

"My mom's turn to entertain the choir," he said, pointing to the other room.

Sarah took off her coat and stood there in the tight faded jeans and the shimmery blue tank top. Dave was taken aback; then he let out a low whistle.

"Don't you look hot," he said slowly.

"Hot for you," she replied. Dave gave her a strange look. "Want to go out tomorrow night?" she went on.

"Yeah, sure. Is this what you'll be wearing then too?" he asked with a grin.

"Maybe," replied Sarah. "So where are you taking me tomorrow?"

"Anywhere you want to—Wait! I almost forgot. I've got that basketball banquet tomorrow."

"So take me with you," said Sarah.

"I can't. I already promised Orchid . . ."

"I knew it!" Sarah snapped. She reached for her coat.

"Now don't start that again," he said, stepping in front of her. "I'm tired of walking on tiptoes around your jealousy."

"I'm not jealous!"

The conversation outside the kitchen hushed momentarily. Sarah and Dave stayed silent until people began chatting again. Then Sarah said calmly, "You keep telling me that you don't like Orchid as a girlfriend and that she gets on your nerves. So why are you spending so much time

94

around her? I just don't get it."

"I'm doing Ray-Ray a favor. She gets stupid around guys. The other day I almost got into a fight with some football players she was flirting with."

"She's an adult, Dave. She doesn't need you to baby-sit her. What is she, twenty–three?" Sarah asked.

"She's nineteen. And she's nowhere near as mature as you are—when you're acting normal."

Sarah stared at him. She could feel her anger melting. And through her tank top she could also feel a cool draft coming from the kitchen door that led outside. She shivered. What a stupid move, she thought. I don't want Dave to like me because I'm wearing this outfit.

"Look, I'd better get back inside," he said. "And by the way, you do look very sexy tonight."

"Nice of you to notice," Sarah said with a tiny smile.

"Yeah, I noticed when I first saw you. If you took off your coat out there, my mom's choir would have had a heart attack!"

Sarah giggled as Dave headed back to his mother's guests. She unlocked the kitchen door that led outside. She didn't want to walk through the living room and confront those strangers again.

As she pulled the door open, she saw Orchid's reflection in the glass. Sarah whirled around and saw her in Dave's T-shirt and the same cutoff shorts he had been wearing last Saturday.

"Oh, you look so cute!" Orchid said. "Almost like a big girl!" Then she gestured at her own outfit. "Dave just loves it when I wear his old clothes." She smiled sweetly. Sarah didn't care if the whole party knew it was her who had slammed the door so hard.

Tasha had only a couple of designs to go, and she was exhausted. She could vaguely picture a pair of long shorts and a blouse to go with them but somehow she couldn't get them down on paper. She started outlining the blouse with her pencil when suddenly she felt a hand rest on her shoulder.

Tasha screamed and whirled around, hitting Allison across the face. Allison fell backwards into her friend Pam and in a moment all three girls were screaming.

"What are you doing?" Tasha yelled. "Why did you sneak up on me like that?"

"I didn't do anything!" Allison was holding the side of her face.

"You did too!" Tasha saw that the half-frame glasses she had been wearing had flown off her face and broken against the bookcase.

"I did not!"

"And look what you've done!" Tasha shrieked as she snatched up the broken glasses.

Allison looked horrified. Pam ran out of the room, almost bumping into Miss Essie.

"Why didn't you knock, Allison?" Tasha yelled. Tears of frustration welled in her eyes. She was more upset about losing the idea than about the glasses.

"What's all this screaming about, Tasha?" Miss Essie demanded.

"I don't have any privacy around here," Tasha yelled back.

"Calm down, girl," Miss Essie warned.

"I just wanted to show Pam what Tasha was doing," Allison blubbered, "and then Tasha hit me!"

"It was an accident!" Tasha retorted. "I wasn't expecting anyone to disrupt me!"

"Allison, you know better than to go into Tasha's room without knocking!" Miss Essie scolded. She looked at Tasha. "And Tasha, you have to remember that there are other people living in this house. You're going to have to live with some interruptions."

Miss Essie led Allison out and closed Tasha's door. Tasha got out of her chair and stomped over to her closet. She yanked her suitcase out, threw it on the floor and began tossing clothes inside. When she was finished she went into the hall and telephoned Jennifer. She had lots of space in that big house of hers.

Sarah slammed the door as she entered the house. She didn't see the Volvo in the driveway, so her parents must still be out. She had to unload her troubles on somebody. She knocked on Tasha's door. "Can I come in for a minute?"

"Sure, what do I care," Tasha grumbled.

Sarah saw Tasha with one knee on her suitcase, trying to get it closed.

"Well, are you going to give me a hand or aren't you?" Tasha said.

Sarah bent down to hold the suitcase shut while Tasha closed the latches. "Whatever happened, it can't be that bad," Sarah said.

"Easy for you to say," Tasha shot back, "they're your family."

"What are you talking about, Tasha? They're your family too."

"Nobody lets me do what I want around here. I've got to get away."

"What will that prove?" Sarah said.

"Maybe nothing," Tasha retorted, "but at least I'll have some peace and quiet." Tasha dragged the suitcase out into the hallway. Sarah watched her punch the redial button on the telephone, then hang up in frustration.

Tasha dragged the suitcase to the top of the steps.

"Look, Tasha. There's no reason to leave," Sarah said, grabbing her arm.

Tasha shook her arm off. For the first time, she noticed that Sarah was wearing one of her sexy tops and her tight jeans. "Why are you dressed like that?"

Sarah burst into tears and ran into her own room,

slamming the door behind her as hard as she could. When the door popped open, she slammed it again, and this time it stayed shut.

Miss Essie's bedroom door flew open. She came out of her room tying the belt of her bathrobe around her waist.

"What is the matter with everybody tonight?" she said in exasperation. Her eye fell on the suitcase.

Tasha went to grab the suitcase, but instead it slipped out of her hand and went crashing down the stairs, hitting the wall and the balusters until it smacked the bottom of the stairs with a loud thump.

The front door opened, and Mr. and Mrs. Gordon walked in. They saw the suitcase in the middle of the foyer and Tasha, Allison, and Miss Essie looking down at them.

"What's going on in here?" Mr. Gordon demanded.

Sarah stuck her head out of her room and everybody started to speak at once. Miss Essie stood in her nightgown pointing at her three granddaughters.

Just then the doorbell rang. When Mrs. Gordon opened it, April walked in with an overnight bag.

"Can I spend the night here, Mrs. Gordon? Just for the night?"

"You can have my bed," Tasha said.

"Does your father know where you are, April?" Mr. Gordon asked.

April shook her head.

"And where are *you* going?" Mrs. Gordon asked Tasha.

"I can't work here. And I have a deadline to meet."

"You've been under too much pressure. That Windmeyer has just worked you too hard," Miss Essie said.

"I could handle the pressure if I got a little cooperation," Tasha cried.

"You'd get more cooperation if you weren't such a prima donna," said Sarah.

Mr. Gordon went to the phone to call April's dad.

"Alice and I had another fight," April explained, answering the curious looks.

"It must have been pretty bad," Sarah said.

"It was awful! They were painting the room they're getting ready for the baby and I knocked over the ladder. I didn't mean to do it. Alice said I did it on purpose."

"I know how you feel," Tasha said. "I hate being blamed for something I didn't do."

"That's enough, Tasha," Mrs. Gordon said.

Tasha drew back at her aunt's tone. She had never heard Mrs. Gordon speak so sternly.

Mr. Gordon came back from the phone. "April, your father agreed to let you stay here for the night," he said. "And he also agreed to let you stay at their house tonight," he said to Tasha. "Why don't you go there instead of disrupting Jennifer's family as well?"

Tasha nodded and picked up her suitcase.

"Leave the suitcase here. It's only for one night," Mr. Gordon ordered. "We're all going to talk about this after school tomorrow."

Mr. Gordon put on his coat again and Tasha followed him out the door.

In the kitchen Sarah poured herself a glass of milk. Mrs. Gordon walked in.

"Sarah," she began, "I know I've been very busy these past few weeks, and I want to say I'm sorry if I haven't been there for you and Tasha."

"Whatever Tasha and I are going through, it's not because of you," Sarah assured her.

"Even so, I just want you to know that I love you and Tasha both very much. And I want you to let me in a little bit. Is there anything wrong?"

"Wrong?" Sarah heard her voice. "No, everything's just fine! I'm fine. Tasha's fine. Dave is fine. And that horrible girl who's actually living in his house and wearing his T-shirt is fine! Everybody's fine!"

"You mean Orchid?" Mrs. Gordon asked.

Sarah grimaced. "Who else?"

"Well, are the two of them . . ." Mrs. Gordon began.

"He says they're not, but the way she's acting—they have to be doing something!" Sarah was almost shouting.

"I can see why you'd suspect the worst." Mrs.

Gordon smiled. "But maybe Dave is telling you the truth. There are lots of girls out there who make themselves very available and lots of guys who don't take them up on it. Have you ever seen Dave and Orchid kissing?"

"No, but you've seen her!" Sarah said. "You see what she's like!"

"Right, but you know what Dave is like, too," Mrs. Gordon said.

"You're telling me to trust him?" asked Sarah.

Mrs. Gordon shrugged. "At least until you know otherwise."

After her mother had gone to bed, Sarah walked to Tasha's door. "You all right, April?" she whispered.

"Yeah, I guess so."

Sarah had heard April crying. Suddenly her problems with Dave didn't seem so bad. At least she had two parents who loved her—and each other. She walked over to the bed and hugged April. "Don't cry, friend," she said. "Everything will look better in the morning."

She held April as she sobbed. Sarah hoped she was right. She hoped everything would look better in the morning.

Eleven

Mrs. Parisi had finally handed back the exams they had taken earlier that week. Next to the small "F" on Tasha's paper she had written, "See me." Tasha stayed in the classroom till the other students had left. Mrs. Parisi closed the door and turned to Tasha.

"I'm very disappointed in you," she said.

Tasha put her head down. It seemed everybody was disappointed in her these days.

"Last week I gave you the benefit of the doubt on that quiz," Mrs. Parisi continued. "But you did much worse than I expected on this test. Didn't I tell you to come to me if you were having a problem with the material?"

Tasha nodded without looking up.

Mrs. Parisi softened her tone. "I'm concerned

about you. You look tired all the time. I heard about the job you're doing for that designer. Is that what's running you ragged?"

Tasha nodded. "It's a great opportunity for me. I don't want to let it go by."

Mrs. Parisi took out a pad of school stationery. She scribbled a few lines on it and handed it to Tasha. "I want to set up a meeting with your aunt and uncle to discuss this with them. Maybe they're not aware just how much time this extra job is taking from your schoolwork."

"Please, Mrs. Parisi," Tasha pleaded. "I promise I'll do better. Don't bring my aunt and uncle into this."

"I'm sorry," said Mrs. Parisi. Tasha saw the firm look in her eyes and knew it was pointless to argue. She took the note and left without a word.

As she walked down the hall to her locker, she saw Mrs. Keiser walking toward her. Tasha tried to duck into the rest room, but the coach called her name.

"Tasha," she said, "you really let the team down last night. It's not fair to the other girls. If your other commitments are going to continue to interfere with games and practices, your only choice is to quit the team."

Again Tasha tried to explain about Mr. Windmeyer and the fashions. The coach cut her off.

"I don't care if the L.A. Lakers want you as a

power forward," she warned. "Don't make me put you off the team." Mrs. Keiser turned and walked away.

At her locker Tasha found a sheet of notebook paper with the score of Murphy High's loss to Rector High on it. "Thanks for nothing," someone had written. She sighed and thought about what Mrs. Keiser had just said. She didn't seem to have a choice.

The day couldn't get any worse, Tasha thought as she pushed open the glass door of 18 Pine St. She was in desperate need of a lift.

Jennifer was showing something in the newspaper to the others. Tasha hoped it was good news.

"Hi, people," she said.

"Hi, cuz," Sarah answered. This was the first time she'd seen her cousin all day.

Tasha gave her a warm smile. "How are things going today?"

"Take a look, Tasha," Jennifer said. She dropped a copy of *The Madison Advocate* on the table. There, in full color, was a picture of Orchid. Her short bangs had been dyed a bright yellow.

"Orchid has been chosen to model for the Windmeyer Company!" said April excitedly. "Story on page B-seven."

"What?" Tasha grabbed the paper and unfolded it. "She doesn't have any experience!"

"I'm not surprised," Jennifer said. "She's got the looks."

"What about her plans to play for Snake Farm?" Cindy asked.

"I guess that's out," April said. "What would you rather do, shake a tambourine for some heavy-metal band and travel in a dirty bus all day, or fly around in jets from Rome to New York for fashion shoots?"

"That's not much of a choice," Jennifer had to admit.

"Did you all see this?" Billy Turner had approached their table. He too held a copy of the Madison newspaper under his arm. He pulled a chair up to their table. "This chick is headed for the big time!"

"Yeah." Tasha fumed. "I'm glad somebody is." She decided to ignore Billy. She turned to April instead. "How did you sleep last night?" she asked.

"Probably like you," said April, laughing. "I kept waking up and wondering where I was."

"You probably thought you were back at my house," Jennifer teased. "You've been wandering all over town lately."

"I'm going to quit that for a while," April said. She told them about the talk she'd had with her father. "He was waiting for me after school today and we went for a long drive. We talked about everything—my real mom, Alice, and the baby on the way."

"Then it went okay?" Tasha asked.

"I think so," April said. "We drove for nearly an

hour. He said that the new baby made him nervous, too. He was worried I would hate the baby just because it was Alice's child! I mean, how could anyone hate a baby?"

"I can see where he'd get that idea," said Jennifer matter-of-factly.

"Be serious, I'm not worried about the baby. It's my stepmother who's the problem," April protested.

"Look, I'm out of here," Billy said, standing. "I got to see a man about a football."

Tasha watched him go. "Isn't that just like a man?" she said. "Soon as things get serious they bug out."

"You going to be all right?" Sarah said.

"I'll be all right," Tasha said finally. "Hey, I'm glad we're on speaking terms again."

"Forget about it," said Sarah. "I knew you were tense about those designs."

"The whole thing is getting on my nerves. Mr. Windmeyer made the deadline sooner, and I can't come up with enough designs that I really like."

"Isn't there some way I can help?" Sarah said. "I can't draw very well, but I could sharpen pencils or something."

Tasha hesitated. She really wanted this to be a Tasha Gordon Production, and she knew she could do it if it weren't for so many distractions. She thought about Mrs. Parisi's note, which was still in her backpack, and the promise she had made to Mr. and Mrs. Gordon about keeping her grades up. The minute she turned over the note, her whole career would come to an end. If she wanted to turn in those sketches before the deadline, she needed help.

"Do you want to knock some ideas around with me?" Tasha said.

"Absolutely!" her cousin replied. They both stood.

"Where are you two going?" April asked.

"We have masterpieces to design," said Tasha.

"I'll go with you," said April. "I still have my suitcase at your place."

At the Gordons', April called her house and asked her father to pick her up. Sarah and Tasha tried to talk with April about her problems at home.

"Maybe you should talk things over with Alice, too," Tasha said.

"I don't know," April replied. "I don't think it will do any good."

They were interrupted by a car horn beeping in the driveway. April grabbed her suitcase and said good-bye. She froze in the doorway, and Tasha and Sarah saw that it wasn't her father in the car.

"That's her," April murmured under her breath.

From the way April had described her, Tasha expected to see a bloated old hag hunched inside the station wagon, clutching the steering wheel with vicious bird claws. Instead they saw a petite woman in her late thirties. She waved when she saw them at the doorway.

"I'd get out of the car," Alice yelled as she unrolled her window, "but it's murder getting back in with this bowling ball I'm carrying."

Sarah and Tasha laughed and walked April down to the car. Alice seemed very pleasant, but April barely acknowledged her. She just got into the passenger seat and stared straight ahead, her teeth clenched. As the Winters backed out of the driveway, Tasha looked at Sarah and shrugged. "I think April has to give Alice a chance. Maybe then the two of them can work things out."

"I agree completely," Sarah answered, putting an arm around her cousin. "But right now you and I have our own work to do."

The two of them hurried inside.

PINE

Twelve

"Colorful, but not tacky," said Sarah.

"Bold, but not obnoxious," Tasha responded.

The cousins were in Tasha's room, pacing across the rug that was strewn with clothing and paper.

"What about a jacket with a paisley print and a rounded collar?" Sarah suggested.

"Yes!" Tasha said, scribbling on her drawing pad. "And some funky bone-type buttons."

They batted ideas back and forth for almost two hours. At one point, Tasha drew a jacket with six-foot sleeves and a football number on the front. "For Billy," she said with a laugh. "The sleeves tie together in back!"

Mr. Gordon finally called them down for dinner.

"You two artistes doing all right? I could hear you brainstorming all the way down in the den."

"Klaus Windmeyer won't know what hit him," said Tasha.

"I meant to ask you about him. Did you see the article in today's paper on your friend Orchid? I keep wondering why Windmeyer keeps hiring first-timers to do his designing and modeling."

"I can answer that for you," said Mrs. Gordon, coming out of the kitchen with a steaming plate of rice. "I've been looking into the Windmeyer Company. Mr. Windmeyer may be eccentric, but he's very shrewd. He often hires local talent from the towns he visits because it's free publicity for him. When a hometown girl is picked to model or design, the local newspapers run a big story." She pointed to the newspaper Mr. Gordon was holding. "A story about Orchid or Tasha is cheaper and more valuable than any advertisement. On top of all that, he doesn't have to pay a new model or designer as much money as a professional one."

"Are you saying he's a crook?" Tasha asked.

"Not as far as I know," Mrs. Gordon assured her. "He just does things his own way."

Allison and her friend Pam walked in. Mr. Gordon nearly dropped his fork when he saw the two of them. They had both combed their hair into bangs and frosted the tips a bright yellow. Sarah clapped her hand over her mouth to keep from laughing.

"What on earth have you two done to your hair?" Mrs. Gordon cried.

Allison sat down and calmly helped herself to some salad. "Just some temporary hair dye," she said. "We got it at the mall. Now we look like Orchid's picture."

"You mean you *want* to look like Orchid?" Tasha laughed.

"She's the next big thing," Pam piped up. "The newspaper said so."

"You'd better pray that stuff comes out, Allison," said Sarah.

"My new name is Alley Cat," Allison declared.

"And I'm Painted Butterfly," said Pam.

"I beg your pardon," Mr. Gordon said.

"We have new names," Allison explained, "just like Orchid changed hers. She used to be called Teri Smith, you know."

"I suppose if Orchid decided to wear socks on her ears, you'd go out and buy a pair?" Mr. Gordon said.

"That would be silly, Daddy," Allison replied.

Miss Essie walked in just then and went to her chair at the end of the table. "Sorry I'm late," she said. "I had to clean the bathroom. What a mess!"

"Mother!" shouted Mr. Gordon. Miss Essie looked at him. Her normally gray hair was streaked with blond wisps that she had combed down over her forehead.

Sarah and Tasha were giggling uncontrollably.

Then Miss Essie announced that she would like to be called Easy Effie.

"What is so funny?" Miss Essie demanded, looking at the older girls, who doubled over, shrieking with laughter.

Mrs. Gordon's smile grew mischievous. "You say that dye washes out, Allison?"

"Now don't you be getting any ideas!" said Mr. Gordon.

"That's Earthy Momma to you," Mrs. Gordon said, shaking her head from side to side.

Mr. Gordon just threw up his hands.

It was almost ten when Sarah and Tasha finally called it quits. They had come up with eighteen sketches. Tomorrow Tasha would decide which twelve to send to Mr. Windmeyer.

"I wish I'd had your help a long time ago," said Tasha, putting her markers in her desk. "Maybe I wouldn't have had to blow off my classes and basketball." She told Sarah about Mrs. Parisi's note and the deal Tasha had made with Mr. Gordon. "If Uncle Donald finds out about the F I got, he'll make me quit. I want to send off the sketches, then see what happens."

"Tasha, you're not still considering dropping out of high school—are you?" Sarah asked.

Tasha shrugged. "Not right now. But this is my big chance, Sarah. I want to go to college, but I may never get another break like this. If Mr. Windmeyer wants more designs, then I want to do them. And I'm not sure I can do both school and designing."

"I wish you'd never met Mr. Windmeyer," Sarah remarked. "I mean, why does an opportunity like this have to cost so much?" She looked worried as she left Tasha's room.

Tasha kicked off her sneakers and stretched out on top of her bed. She closed her eyes, letting pictures of the world of fashion drift through her mind. Gone were her images of expensive parties and handsome photographers. Now she imagined photographers who were as old as Mr. Windmeyer, and the gorgeous male models were as stuck-up as Orchid was. So far designing clothes was not nearly as glamorous as Tasha had always dreamed it was.

Tasha dozed off on top of her bed. She jumped when Mr. Gordon knocked on her door and said there was a phone call for her. It couldn't be one of her friends. They knew better than to call the house after 9:30. Maybe it was Mr. Windmeyer.

The British accent was unmistakable. "Is this Tasha?" Orchid said. Tasha gave her a groggy reply. "Sorry to call so late. I didn't expect you to be in bed on a Friday night. Anyway," she went on, "I'm calling to tell you to be at the Westcove Mall tomorrow. As you must know, I'm modeling the new collection—but you must have seen the paper, no? Anyway, Ms. Tique is going to have a special private showing of Windmeyer's spring line."

"I'd love to, but I can't." Tasha didn't even bother to pretend she was regretful. "I have plans tomorrow. Besides, I'm not working on that collection. I'm doing the Def Soul Casuals line. I'm about to send my sketches to Mr. Windmeyer."

"Actually, there's been a change in plans," Orchid said haughtily. "Klaus told me to have you there. He wants you to show your sketches to his representatives, to give them an idea of what you're doing."

Tasha put her hand over the mouthpiece of the phone so that her groan wouldn't be heard.

"Be at Ms. Tique at four o'clock," Orchid snapped, as if she was used to giving orders. "Remember, Klaus's agent wants to see what you've come up with so far."

The phone clicked before Tasha could even start to protest. One thing about Orchid, she thought. The girl made it easy to hate her.

PINE

Thirteen

On Saturday morning Sarah went to the front door to get the newspaper and found an envelope with her name written on it wedged against the handle. Inside was a note from Dave: "Truce?—D." She put the note in her pocket and walked into the kitchen with the newspaper. She remembered her visit to his house, and the sight of Orchid in his clothes. No way, she thought bitterly. She pulled the note out of her pocket and crumpled it into a tight ball as she flipped to the comics page.

Yesterday she had tried to avoid seeing Dave all day, but it was almost impossible. When their biology class went on a field trip to the aquarium on the outskirts of Madison, Sarah found that the only seat left on the bus was next to him. Had he planned it

116

that way? she wondered. He was acting friendly, but Sarah stayed aloof until he got the message and turned to look out the window. When they reached the aquarium, Dave stayed in the back of the tour group and Sarah kept close to the teacher.

"Put him out of your mind," she said to herself sternly. She repeated it a minute later when she found herself wondering how his speech had gone at the sports dinner.

Tasha and Sarah spent the afternoon at the mall, waiting for four o'clock. There was a sign posted near the entrance of Ms. Tique announcing that it was closing early for the showing of the Windmeyer spring line. The girls wandered up and down the row of shops and ended up in the record store. They were debating splitting the cost of the latest Def Cru 4 cassette when they heard familiar voices.

Kwame and Steve approached them, and Orchid was with them. She wore tight black jeans that hugged her thighs and a tight gold-colored turtleneck that hugged everything else.

"I hope that outfit cuts her circulation off and she passes out," Tasha muttered to her cousin.

Steve had a silly grin on his face, but Kwame seemed to be immune to Orchid's spell.

"We saw Orchid hitchhiking and picked her up," said Steve. An awkward silence followed. Suddenly Orchid let out a wail and reached into a

CD bin. She pulled out the latest Snake Farm release and stared at the colorful cover.

"What am I going to do?" she cried. "Snake Farm is coming to town on Friday, and I'm supposed to go to New York City to meet with Mr. Windmeyer that day. Snake Farm is expecting me to play with them."

"Just tell Snake Farm you changed your mind," said Kwame.

"I guess I'll have to," said Orchid with a pout. "But it won't be easy. Music is my first love."

Orchid is your first love, thought Sarah. She could have kissed Kwame when she saw him roll his eyes at Orchid's remark.

"Are those your designs?" Orchid asked Tasha, pointing at the notebook under her arm.

"What else would they be, Orchid?" Tasha answered sweetly, pulling Sarah away. "We'll see you later at Ms. Tique," she called back.

"I'll go with you," said Orchid, walking after them. "Thanks for the ride, Steve, it was really nice of you."

Steve's grin widened. "Do you need a ride home?"

"No," said Orchid, "but you're sweet to ask."

When Orchid caught up with the girls, she tapped Sarah on the shoulder. "You *do* know that the viewing is for models, designers, and buyers only."

118

"Good thing she's a codesigner," Tasha said, walking faster.

As the three walked past the food court, Sarah nudged Tasha and pointed out April and Alice Winter. They were huddled together in what looked like an intense conversation. Then the girls saw April actually throw back her head and laugh. She caught sight of the Gordons and waved them over.

"We'll catch you later," Tasha told Orchid firmly.

Alice looked a little tired, but she smiled warmly at them. "Would you like some calamari?" She pointed at a basket of something that looked like curly fried potatoes.

"Don't let the name fool you, it's fried squid! Alice gets cravings for seafood," April explained with a smile.

"Yes," Alice said, "I'm worried the baby will become a scuba diver." Her eye fell on the portfolio Tasha was carrying and the cousins explained about the private showing. Alice asked if she could see the designs. Tasha resisted at first, but finally handed the portfolio to her. She turned the pages slowly, then looked at the Gordons with sincere admiration. "You make a great designing team," she said. "Now I can say I knew you when."

At Ms. Tique's there was lots of activity. Tasha and Sarah hurried into the store, brushing past the salesclerk, who was trying to get the store closed down and prevent any more shoppers from entering.

Several clothes racks had been pushed aside to clear an open space next to the changing room. Sarah and Tasha were the youngest of the thirty or so people who milled around a table brimming with Dutch cheeses, sparkling water, and white wine. Others were seated in the chairs that lined the walls of the store. A small runway area had been created in the center. Orchid and one other model were bustling around in the changing area, getting ready for the show.

A small, neat-looking man with a thin mustache quieted everyone down. He introduced himself as Mr. Helming, a representative of the Windmeyer collection of fine women's wear. Tasha gripped her portfolio to her chest. Would a man like him be impressed by Def Soul Casuals?

The two models alternated showing the clothes. They wore different outfits and wigs each time they came out. This time Orchid didn't cause a sensation, though she looked great. The buyers nodded appreciatively or shook their heads. As they took notes, Sarah tried to figure out which outfits they liked and didn't like. The gowns and dresses were, as far as Sarah was concerned, just more of the same old things—lot of rhinestones and beads and bangles.

Mr. Helming had a small microphone clipped to his tie, and he announced each piece, describing it from memory. When all the clothing had been modeled, he sat and talked to the prospective buyers. A reporter, Sarah noticed, was asking Orchid a barrage of questions. She'd probably bring Mr. Windmeyer even more publicity. Just wait till Tasha's designs are in production, Sarah thought with excitement. Then Tasha will turn some heads too.

Tasha was waiting patiently for Mr. Helming to finish with the buyers. She was eager to show him her sketches and leave as soon as possible. But he didn't seem to be in the least bit of a hurry to see them. He talked at length to each buyer, and passed out business cards. When he was finally through with the buyers and packing his attaché case, Tasha made her way up to him and held out the sketches.

"What's this?" Mr. Helming said, gesturing at the portfolio. He didn't try to hide his annoyance.

"I'm working on the Def Soul Casuals line in the Windmeyer Company," Tasha began.

"Oh, yes, yes, of course," he said, glancing at his watch. "Mr. Windmeyer told me about you. You're supposed to be quite good. Didn't he tell you that he wants the other young lady—Orchid—to look at the sketches? After all she'll be the one wearing them. You'll send him copies, naturally, and she'll send along her opinion as well. All part of keeping in touch with the pulse of American youth. It's been charming meeting you."

"But I thought I was supposed to show my sketches to you," Tasha said.

"I am not here in that capacity," Mr. Helming said stiffly. "Now if you will excuse me . . ." He turned back to the buyers for a last good-bye and was out the door.

Tasha couldn't believe it. Why had Mr. Windmeyer decided that Orchid should be the one to look at the sketches? It made no sense at all. Fighting back tears of rage and frustration, she marched over to Orchid. She turned away as the thin girl, still dressed in a gold two-piece outfit with a bare midriff, flipped through the sketches.

"Mmmm . . . nice . . . oh . . . oh, dear . . . oh, dear—"

Tasha had had enough. "Give me that!" she demanded, grabbing her portfolio.

"You have one or two good pieces," Orchid said. "I liked the shoulder lines in particular, but the rest of it is a little . . . ordinary. Don't you think so?"

Tasha gave her an icy stare.

"And look at this." Orchid opened the portfolio and pointed to the sketch at the top of the pile and pretended to suppress a laugh. "Do you really think those black baggy shorts would go with a tight chemise? I'd look lopsided in something like that."

"What do you know about designing?" Tasha said hotly. "You're just a model."

"I don't have to 'know.' I can feel they're wrong."

"Let's go," Sarah said, pulling her cousin away. She saw they were attracting attention.

122

Steve and Kwame were standing by the big picture window in the front of Ms. Tique.

"Didn't you hear Orchid tell you she had a ride?" Tasha snapped.

"We were waiting for you," Steve mumbled.

Tasha didn't say a word.

"How did it go?" He tried again once they were in the car.

"Let's not talk about it," suggested Sarah. "Kwame, how's that report going? Weren't you writing about blacks in a war?"

"In a war? Oh, yeah, man the guns!" he said. "We are still talking about the Revolutionary War, aren't we?"

"What else!" Tasha snapped.

Kwame talked about the surprising number of black heroes he had found. Sarah noticed that Tasha wasn't listening. She just stared out the window at the mall. One of the movies had just ended, and the line of cars waiting to leave the parking lot was longer than usual. Steve's car idled near the back of a stream of cars waiting for the light to change. Suddenly Sarah saw Tasha's face take on a look of surprise. She followed Tasha's eyes and saw Orchid and a boy standing near the mall entrance; they were locked in a passionate embrace.

"That girl has zero class," Tasha said with disgust.

Finally the couple pulled apart. The lights in the parking lot lit the front of the mall like a stage. As

Steve put his battered Toyota in gear, Sarah suddenly recognized the boy who had been kissing Orchid.

It was Dave!

PINE

Fourteen

Sunday went by in a blur. The numb sensation Sarah had felt since Saturday night at the Westcove Mall had not diminished. She was surprised she didn't feel like crying; she just felt empty. It was as if the war was over and Orchid had won.

The Federal Express envelope was on the coffee table when Sarah and Tasha got home from school on Monday.

"Windmeyer wants the final sketches sent on Tuesday!" Tasha wailed as she crumpled letter inside the package.

"But we're finished," Sarah said.

"No we're not!" said Tasha vehemently. She picked up the portfolio from the coffee table where she had dropped it on Saturday night and carried it into the kitchen. Then Sarah heard paper tearing.

"Are you crazy?" Sarah shrieked as she ran in. She tried to grab the remaining sketches from Tasha's hands.

"Leave me alone, Sarah, I know what I'm doing." Tasha went on ripping each sheet. "I'm not going to send him anything that *she* saw." Tasha had had doubts about the quality of her work, and Orchid's comments had made them worse. She had picked apart every design in her head, and decided that she hated all of them.

"Are you going to let that girl get under your skin? Since when does it matter what she thinks?"

"It doesn't," Tasha said. She looked at Sarah. "And I'm going to do them on my own. Mr. Windmeyer hired Tasha Gordon to give him a Def Soul line, and that's what I'm going to do. I'm going to create a line that he is guaranteed to love."

"You want to start from scratch?" Sarah was incredulous. "Those sketches nearly wiped you out."

"I can do it," Tasha said firmly.

"And you don't want me to help you?"

"Hey, cuz, you helped. It made a difference. But these have got to be mine alone," Tasha said. "I think I need to do it. No hard feelings, okay?"

"Okay, Tasha," Sarah said. "I just hope you know what you're doing."

Sarah went to her room and tried to concentrate on her homework. Finally she threw her pencil down and walked to Tasha's room.

"There's still time," she said. "We can tape those sketches together and I can help you copy them."

"Thanks, Sarah," said Tasha without looking up. "I'll have them done by tomorrow."

PINE

Fifteen

For the third time Miss Essie knocked on Tasha's door. It was seven in the morning, and although Tasha was never a cheerful riser, Miss Essie could usually expect a grunt in reply on the second knock. She peered in and saw the empty bed. Tasha was slumped over the her desk.

"Girl, are you all right?" Miss Essie shook her softly.

Tasha raised her head. Her elbow stuck to the sheet of sketches and she looked around with confused eyes.

"What time is it?"

"Time for you to go to school," Miss Essie said.

Tasha looked at the clock. "I slept for half an hour," she said. She stood up, her muscles complaining from the effort. She rubbed her eyes and focused on her grandmother.

"Is she all right?" said Sarah from the door.

"You go on to school," Miss Essie said. "Tasha is sick."

"I'm not sick," Tasha protested. "I just need a shower."

"You haven't had any sleep, and you're sick in the head for staying up all night. You're of no use to anyone in that condition," Miss Essie said, guiding Tasha back to the bed.

Tasha knew better than to argue with Miss Essie once she had made up her mind.

She lay on the bed after Sarah and Miss Essie had left, but she didn't feel drowsy. "I'm too tired to sleep," she said aloud. She got up and went to the sketchpad, flipping through the designs she had drawn the night before. They were bold, unusual, and very powerful-looking clothes. One piece in particular stood out. It was a skirt and blouse that looked like a flowing African dress but also had pants under the skirt. When the skirt came off the outfit looked almost Spanish. She barely remembered drawing a few of the sketches. She spent some time transferring them to clean sheets of paper and coloring them in carefully. She'd been ravenously hungry when she finally finished.

Mrs. Gordon, who had come back to the house to pick up some court briefs, was surprised to see

Tasha at home.

"Aren't you feeling well?"

Tasha smiled. "I thought I was, but Miss Essie didn't agree." She put her sketches in the large white envelope Mr. Windmeyer had sent.

"Do you mind if I take a look at them?" Mrs. Gordon said. Tasha reluctantly handed the unsealed mailing packet to her aunt. Orchid had done a good job of hurting Tasha's confidence. The trouble with fashion design, she realized, was that everybody had a different idea what good taste was. More and more she was doubting her own ideas and creations.

Mrs. Gordon went through the sheets one by one. She didn't change the expression on her face as she looked them over. Finally, when she had seen them all, she shuffled the sheets straight and fastened the clips to the corner.

"They're wonderful," she said simply. "If you'd like me to, I'll take them to my office. I can make copies and mail them from there."

Tasha started to cry. She felt ridiculous—she was punchy from lack of sleep, but she couldn't control herself. Mrs. Gordon wrapped her arms around her and just held her for a few minutes.

Tasha slept until late that afternoon. She walked into the kitchen and saw Sarah wiping the counter dry.

"How's Sleeping Beauty?" Sarah asked.

"Fine," Tasha said, opening the refrigerator. She pulled out the chicken salad Sarah had just put away and ate it standing over the sink.

"I saw the sketches," Sarah said. "Mom said they were wonderful and they are!"

"She brought the copies home?" Tasha put two slices of rye bread in the toaster.

"And she couldn't wait to show them off. She's so proud of you," Sarah said. "You must be so happy with them."

"I don't know," Tasha said. "I know I tried very hard. It was the best I could do under the circumstances."

"Are you still upset about Orchid?" Sarah asked.

"No way!" Tasha sniffed. "Well . . . maybe. It kills me that she has the looks and the style that I'm supposed to be designing for."

"She's definitely put together, you have to admit that," Sarah said miserably.

Tasha looked at her cousin. "I'm sorry you had to see Dave with her."

Sarah's eyes welled with tears. She pulled the kitchen stepladder out and sat on it. "I haven't been able to tell you all the details because you've been so busy. Dave seems really attracted to her. I just can't compete with a girl like Orchid."

"That's not true!" her cousin said. "You've got much more going for you than she does."

"Nothing the boy's going to notice," Sarah said.

"Matter of fact, nothing I've noticed, either."

"Well, that tells you something about Dave, doesn't it?" said Tasha. "You're beautiful, you're smart, you're considerate, you've got class. You're much more interesting to be around than that . . . that mannequin!" Tasha's eyes lit up mischievously. "Why, you're almost as wonderful as I am."

Sarah smiled slightly. "I'll be glad when Orchid moves on to whatever big time she's going to be moving on to."

"You're not the only one!" Tasha agreed.

PINE

Sixteen

Tasha was in homeroom when she heard the announcement over the PA system inviting everybody to come to the next girls' basketball game. She wondered if she would play. Two days had passed since she sent the envelope of sketches to Mr. Windmeyer, and she still hadn't had a reply. She had attacked her books and basketball practice with renewed intensity, but the days she had missed had taken their toll. Her passing wasn't working at all.

That evening another Federal Express package was waiting for Tasha on the coffee table. She tore it open eagerly when she saw the Windmeyer logo on the back of the envelope.

A check for $1,200 was fastened to a letter.

Dearest Tasha:

I received your sketches today and was overjoyed by their obvious quality.

At this time, however, your concepts do not fit in with our vision of the Def Soul Casuals line.

We will keep your sketches on file in case we consider them for a future line. In the meantime, I hope you will share with me the pleasure I have in introducing the Def Soul Casuals line in the enclosed brochure.

Sincerely,
K.W.

Tasha looked at the enclosed brochure with disgust. The model was wearing cutesy bright clothing with cartoon animal motifs. There was nothing def or soul about it!

"Fashion designer Kristen MacGriff comes from the small town of Delmont," the brochure read. "Only thirteen years of age, Kristen has a fashion sense that is ahead of her time. Another of Mr. Windmeyer's young discoveries!"

Sarah came in and saw the tears on her cousin's face. Tasha handed her the letter and went to her room.

"According to the contract," Mrs. Gordon told

Tasha at dinner, "you were paid for each part of the development of the line. Your sketches were worth one hundred dollars apiece. He didn't cheat you."

Tasha didn't reply. She couldn't eat either. "Is it okay if I just excuse myself?" she asked.

Mr. and Mrs. Gordon exchanged glances. "Sure, honey," her uncle said.

Later Mr. Gordon found his niece in the den flipping through a fashion magazine.

"I feel so stupid," she said, throwing the magazine on the floor.

"Nothing to feel stupid about," Mr. Gordon said gently. "You gave it your best shot. It just wasn't what they were looking for."

"But I really wanted this to work out."

"Tasha, what if it had worked out?" Mr. Gordon said. "What if Mr. Windmeyer loved your line and you went to work for him? You could have quit school and everything. Then what if he didn't like your next line? You'd be sixteen years old with no job and no diploma."

"I'd look for work in another company," Tasha said stubbornly.

Mr. Gordon shook his head. "Do you think another more traditional company would hire you over men and women who have honed their talents in fashion institutes and art schools?"

"No," Tasha admitted glumly. "I guess I don't have enough talent."

"Whoa, girl, I never said that," Mr. Gordon said as he picked up the magazine. "I think you're extremely talented. That's why you should stay in school: to develop your talent. After college you're on your own. It gets much harder then. Ask anybody. Ask your aunt. Ask me. By the way," Mr. Gordon added, "I like Tasha Gordon the outgoing student and star basketball player more than Tasha Gordon the famous fashion designer. She's more fun."

Tasha sat for a minute and let her uncle's words sink in. "Thanks," she said softly. "You're not going to like this, but there's something I have to show you." She went up to her room and took the note from Mrs. Parisi out of her bookbag.

When Mr. Gordon read it, he frowned. "How long have you been holding on to this?" he asked quietly.

Tasha told him. "I knew you'd never let me finish the job once you saw the note," she added.

Mr. Gordon was silent for a moment. He looked away and shook his head. "You're grounded, Tasha," he said simply. "For the next week. You come home right after basketball practice, you hear?" He stood up. "Not because you failed the test, but because you didn't trust me with this." He waved the note.

Tasha nodded without looking up.

"Now go on upstairs and crack your history book," he ordered, his voice slightly less hard.

PINE

Seventeen

The coach blew her whistle so close to the bench Tasha nearly jumped. She was sitting there with her team jacket thrown over her shoulders as she watched Murphy High struggle against Manlius High School. Ordinarily an easy school for the Murphy squad to beat, the Manlius team was playing above its level and was ahead by three points in the fourth quarter.

"Gordon, go in for Adele," the coach growled.

"Come on, Tasha," Cindy yelled from the bleachers as Tasha removed her jacket and signaled the replacement.

Tasha couldn't shake her nervousness as she ran to the player she was guarding, a tall white girl with plastic goggles. Stop thinking, she told herself, just play.

Goggles suddenly faked a forward charge, stepped back, and got the ball. Tasha stepped in to try to block her shot and got a fingertip on it. The ball fell out of Goggle's hands and rolled toward the outside line. Tasha was on it in a flash. She dribbled to the basket and saw a red jersey wide open. Looking at Goggles, she threw the ball over her shoulder.

The crowd's "awww" told her that her much-practiced over-the-shoulder pass had missed, and Manlius had gained possession of the ball. She saw Goggles smile and head toward her own basket. Tasha kept on her for three more plays, and then was taken out of the game.

The Manlius players took the game into overtime, but the physically stronger Murphy team finally wore them down. When the buzzer went off, the score was 90 to 88, and Tasha jumped up and down with the rest of the team. They'd won a tight game, though mostly due to luck.

"They don't get much closer than that," Mrs. Keiser said back in the locker room. "Listen up, girls. Next week is Ridgefield and if we play like we did today, we're going to get our butts kicked. Gordon, you mind staying a little later for practice next week?"

"No," said Tasha. Coach had said it in a way that gave her no choice. She picked up her gym bag and joined her friends back in the gymnasium.

"Nice game," Kwame commented.

"Oh, please!" said Tasha. Everybody laughed.

"It's really cool of your parents to have us over," Steve told April later. They'd all gone to April's house after the game to hang out and get something to eat.

"Yeah," said April, "things are a lot better. My stepmother is trying a lot harder to include me in stuff and I've decided to make an effort with her too."

Sarah was glad to hear this. Tasha was still grounded, but she'd be happy for April, too, when Sarah filled her in at home.

Sarah was sitting next to Jennifer on the thick carpeted floor of the Winters' den. As they waited for the Chinese food to arrive, they argued with Kwame and José about who the strangest teacher at Murphy High was.

"Mr. Galloway sings to himself," Jennifer remarked. "He is so weird."

"Remember Mr. Lee? He got so mad at one kid, he slammed his hand on the desk and broke two fingers," said April.

"Mrs. Faubus," said José. "She substituted for my math teacher. She kept putting problems on the board to show us how to work them out, but she could never get the right answers. It didn't bother

her, though. She just kept smiling and erasing that blackboard."

April got up to answer the doorbell with the money for the Chinese food. Sarah went with her to help to carry the food. They were both surprised to see Billy Turner at the door, trying to catch his breath. He had left his car out front with the engine running.

"Hurry!" he yelled. "We have to get downtown!"

"What's up?" Sarah asked. "What are you talking about?"

"Dave is getting ready to come to blows with some guys from out of town," Billy said. "We need all the help we can get!"

Jennifer, Cindy, and Sarah got into Billy's car while Steve drove Kwame, José, and April. They headed as fast as they could to downtown Madison.

They pulled into the nearly abandoned parking lot outside the Madison Armory and raced to the back of the building. An enormous bus with a fat snake painted on the side was backed up against the Armory wall and hemmed in there by Dave Hunter's car. The engine of the bus was idling.

"I'm not moving until I talk to her!" Dave yelled as the bus driver honked at him.

Billy got out of his car. Dave ran over to him just as a short, burly man with muttonchop sideburns and stringy red hair came out of the Armory. He had on sunglasses even though it was nighttime, and he

140

wore black leather pants and a leather vest. One arm was draped over Orchid's shoulder. She was wearing black leather pants and a frilly red lace shirt under a black leather jacket. Her face was barely visible under a silver-studded black leather cap. She tottered slightly as her heels clicked across the parking lot.

"Orchid, let's go home!" Dave yelled.

"Are you crazy?" Orchid said. Her British accent was gone. "This is what I came to Madison for. Everybody, this is Stain."

The man with the muttonchops grinned. "Charmed," he said in a gravelly voice. "Now, would you mind getting your cars out of the way?"

Billy stepped forward, clenching and unclenching his fists and towering over Stain. "We're not moving anything until we talk to Orchid."

Stain's arm flexed and rippled slightly. He gripped Orchid even tighter. "It's up to the lady," he growled. "So why don't you just move the car before you get hurt."

"Billy, don't be a child," Orchid said. "There's nothing to talk about. They let me in the band!"

Dave looked at Cindy, Jennifer, and Sarah. "Say something," he said urgently. "She's messed up. You can't just watch her get on that bus."

"What about the modeling?" Sarah said. "I thought that's what you wanted."

Orchid giggled. "I got a better offer," she said.

141

They heard angry voices from inside the bus. The driver honked his horn, and Stain moved forward again. But Billy didn't step aside.

"For the last time, get out of my way!" Stain bellowed.

Billy swung his fist, but Stain ducked the punch and hit Billy in the stomach. Billy doubled over, gasping for air. Dave strode toward Stain with his fists clenched. A skinny band member ran down the steps of the bus holding a large empty wine bottle like a club.

"Dave!" Sarah cried.

Dave stopped and held his ground, his eyes fixed on the man with the bottle.

"Let her go, Dave," Billy gasped.

"That's right," Orchid said. "She's a very big girl, and she doesn't need two little boys protecting her."

Dave took a deep breath and slowly exhaled. Then he got behind the wheel of his car and backed it away from the bus.

They stayed in the parking lot until the bus had disappeared from sight.

Dave drove Sarah and Cindy back to April's house. When he pulled up in front of the Winters', he grabbed Sarah's arm to hold her back as the others went inside.

"Can we talk?" Dave said.

"You mean now that Orchid's run off with Snake Farm?" said Sarah. "Now that your heart is broken?"

"Look, Sarah, I know I was wrong with her," Dave said. "There was never anything between us but . . ."

"But what?" Sarah asked.

The half moon in the dark sky carved shadows along the street. It was growing cold and Sarah shivered slightly.

"Look," Dave said. "Orchid is like . . . really sexy. Half the time I was totally annoyed at her. But sometimes"—he paused—"she is sort of exciting to be around—"

"More exciting than I am, of course," Sarah said. Now she was feeling more angry than cold.

"In a way, yes," Dave answered softly. "I realize that Orchid has a lot of problems. She was using me—using every guy in fact—as a way of dealing with her confusion. I'm just sorry that I got fooled by her act."

Sarah stared at Dave, not saying anything.

"I didn't lie to you, Sarah. Until last Saturday, we never kissed, nothing. It was just for that one moment. Sarah, I care for you so much . . . and in ways I could never care for her. I even think that you know that. Orchid's like a here and now thing. I'm not saying I was right to be interested in her, even for one day, but . . ."

"But now that she's gone you're going to be interested in me again, huh?"

"You make this sound bad," Dave said.

143

"Why don't you go home, Dave," Sarah said. "And take her picture from under your pillow and tell her your sad story. Okay?"

"Hey, wait a minute! Orchid put that picture under my pillow. And in my closet, and in my bookbag. She put pictures of herself all over the house. She even moved my great-grandfather's portrait. Mom was furious."

"Did you let her wear your clothes?"

"She took them out of my room. She didn't care. She was jealous of you, Sarah. She wanted to make you mad."

"What about that kiss?" Sarah said softly. "I saw the two of you outside the mall. Did she grab you and twist your arm?"

Dave looked away. "I was just telling you about that," he said.

"You don't have any excuses?" asked Sarah.

Dave shook his head. Sarah turned to go, and he grabbed her arm again. "I was mad at you," he said. "You kept freezing me out at school, and you never let me explain. I guess I figured since you were mad at me anyway . . ." His voice died off.

"Why didn't you tell me all this sooner?" said Sarah after a long silence.

"Because I wasn't doing anything wrong. I kept waiting for you to come around," he said.

"Well, you just keep waiting," she said, opening the car door. She headed toward April's house.

Eighteen

On Monday morning, Sarah found a piece of note-book paper in Dave's handwriting: "Date? D."

She wrote a note: "No. S.," and put it in his locker.

She knew Dave had told her the truth that night in April's driveway. Tasha didn't see what the problem was when Sarah told her about it.

"Sounds like he wants to get back together with you."

"I know. But I can't face him. I had such strong feelings when I saw the two of them together. I guess I have to let that fade a bit."

"That's how I feel about Billy," Tasha agreed. "Even though he has been a lot nicer to me since that night, just seeing what a fool Orchid turned him into

145

made me realize that he's not the man for me. Boy, that Orchid really kicked up a fuss when she was here."

Sarah nodded.

Mr. Cala was writing questions on the overhead projector when Sarah saw a teammate of Dave's holding up a sign for her to read.

SARAH, GIVE DAVE A BREAK!

On her way to gym class, a boy she knew from Ku'Umba Choir swerved in front of her. He had a sign taped to his backpack.

DAVE IS SORRY. HOW ABOUT IT, SARAH?

There were five other signs, some posted on doors, others being carried by friends of Dave. They made Sarah smile, but she really wanted to cry . . . with happiness. It felt wonderful that Dave cared that much.

He was waiting for her at her locker at the end of the day.

"Did you run out of messengers?" she teased.

"Oh, you saw them?" he said, pretending to sound surprised. His mood turned serious. "Can we be friends again?"

Sarah looked into his rich brown eyes. "Okay," she said. "Friends. Anything more, you'll have to work for."

Dave smiled, took her in his arms, and kissed her.

Sarah kissed him back, then pushed him away for

a second to give him a questioning look. "Better than Orchid?" she asked.

Dave gave her a blank look. "Orchid who?"

Nineteen

Outside 18 Pine St., the wind howled. Sarah rubbed her hands to warm them as she and Tasha entered the pizzeria and headed for their usual table in the back, where everybody else was already gathered.

They had just come back from Mother Belva's Home. There Tasha had turned over $500 of the money Mr. Windmeyer had given her. The rest she put in the bank—except $30. "Let's go to 18 Pine and have a blowout," she'd said.

Technically, Tasha was still grounded, but Mr. Gordon had given her a one-day reprieve when he heard about the donation to Mother Belva. "Those young women at Mother Belva's can use all the help they can get," he had commented.

When Mr. Harris came over with two large pizzas with everything on them, Tasha caught Steve checking his wallet. "It's okay. Dig in," she said. "I got paid."

After finishing his third slice, Kwame cleared his throat loudly and stood up. "I propose a toast. To a member of our group who has gone through a lot of stress and anxiety in the last two weeks, and came out better for it."

"I couldn't have done it without my friends," April said bashfully.

"April!" Jennifer said. "He's referring to Tasha."

"I thought he meant Sarah," said Tasha.

"Actually, I was referring to me," Kwame grumbled. "I finally turned in the paper on the black Revolutionary War heroes."

"Oh, you found some?" Jennifer said.

"Dozens!" Kwame said proudly. He whipped out a sheet of names and began to read them off: "Samuel Torn, Isias Farrow, Isaac Townes, Jonathan Niles, Samuel DeBoevre, Crispus Attucks, Alfred Millman . . ." When he looked up, he noticed the gang was trying to sneak away.

"Hey!" he said.

Steve laughed. "We just wanted to see how long you would go before you noticed."

Suddenly Tasha wailed, "I'm stuck!" She'd tried to slip between two tables when she felt a tug on her leg. Her pants had snagged on something and pinned her to the spot.

Sarah and Jennifer tried to get her free.

149

"I see it!" Jennifer said. "It's a small nail. Don't wiggle, Tasha."

Tasha froze in her awkward position. "These pants cost a fortune," she moaned. "Don't let them tear!"

"You might have to take them off," José said with a grin.

"Oh, eat your jalapeños!" Cindy exclaimed. She crouched down beside Sarah and Jennifer. A few moments later, they heard the fabric rip and Tasha winced audibly.

Sarah had assessed the situation. "There's only one option, Tasha." She moved to shield her cousin from José, Steve, and Kwame's eyes. "Just unbutton them," she whispered.

Steve overheard her. "Yeah, go ahead," he said helpfully, "the place is nearly empty anyway. Besides we won't look, will we, Kwame?"

Kwame put the list of names back into his notebook. He couldn't understand his friends sometimes. What was more important, he thought, Black American history, or Tasha Gordon in her underwear?

But he stuck around. Just in case.

Coming in Book 7,
Intensive Care

Jennifer heard voices. When she opened her eyes, she saw a skinny blond man with a bushy mustache. She became conscious of the rain pelting her face. They had taken her out of the car.

"Can you hear me?" the man asked.

Jennifer moved her head slightly. A woman carrying a medical bag smiled at her. "You're going to be okay."

"What about Sarah?" Jennifer said thickly.

"Don't talk," the woman commanded. Jennifer felt pressure on her chest, hips, and thighs. They had strapped her body to a stiff board.

When Jennifer's mom goes out of town, Jennifer can't resist borrowing her new Saab, even though she only has a learner's permit. But Jennifer's joy ride becomes a terrible nightmare when she and Sarah are involved in a terrible accident. Now Sarah's in a coma, and it's all Jennifer's fault. . . .